Adrian Richard Alington was born in Oxford in 1895, the son of the Reverend E. H. Alington. The First World War broke out just as Alington was finishing his schooling, and from Marlborough College he went straight into the army. He served with the Wiltshire Regiment as a Captain until he was wounded in 1918, and was the Cipher Officer for the Supreme War Council at Versailles.

While serving in France, Alington wrote *What Every General Knows, or Sweet Fanny Adams*, a satirical play which was put on for the troops. Harold Raymond, a fellow officer and a partner in the publishing firm of Chatto & Windus, commissioned Alington after the performance to write a novel; *Slowbags and Arethusa*, his first, was published shortly after the war.

Alington wrote seventeen novels in all, as well as numerous radio scripts, and he edited John Buchan's *Episodes of the Great War*. He also wrote several screenplays, including an adaptation of his own novel, *Those Kids From Town Again*. *The Amazing Test Match Crime*, his tenth novel, was originally published in 1939.

Adrian Alington died in 1958.

THE AMAZING TEST MATCH CRIME

Adrian Alington

*New Introduction by
Brian Johnston*

THE HOGARTH PRESS

LONDON

To S. E. Trotter, Esq.

Published in 1984 by
The Hogarth Press
40 William IV Street, London WC2N 4DF

First published in Great Britain by Chatto & Windus 1939
Hogarth edition offset from original Chatto & Windus edition
Copyright the Estate of Adrian Alington
Introduction copyright © Brian Johnston 1984

British Library Cataloguing in Publication Data
Alington, Adrian
The Amazing Test Match Crime
I. Title
823'912[F] PR6001.L4
ISBN 0 7012 0561 X

Printed in Great Britain by
Cox & Wyman Ltd
Reading, Berkshire

INTRODUCTION

I thought that I had read all the best cricket novels – *England Their England* by A. G. Macdonell, *The Cricket Match* by Hugh de Selincourt, *Mike* by P. G. Wodehouse, *That Test Match* by Sir Home Gordon, *A Sky-Blue Life* by Maurice Moisevitsch, *Mortimer Also* by Jo Rice, and two thrillers: *Death Before Wicket* by Nancy Spain and *Testkill* by Ted Dexter. But *The Amazing Test Match Crime* is one out of the bag. It was first published by Chatto and Windus in 1939, and is now happily republished. I admit I had never heard of Adrian Alington, author of some fifteen books. It seems that he was a nephew of the more famous Dr Cyril Alington, headmaster of Eton in my time and later Dean of Durham, who also wrote books including *Mr Evans – a Cricketer* – a detective story.

There is no evidence that Adrian Alington even played cricket but I am sure he must have done so. He certainly knew all about the game and everyone and everything associated with it. Even more certain is that he loved it. His book is an affectionate parody of those who play, watch and administer cricket and even those who broadcast it. I can quite honestly say that I have never laughed so much at a book since I read about that classic cricket match in *England Their England*. But that was only a small section of a book. This time my laughter and chuckles have continued for nearly two hundred and fifty pages – from the very first over through to close of play.

The story is a simple one. An international gang called The Bad Men plan to disrupt the British Empire by interfering with the fifth and vital Test in a series between England and Imperia. The leader of the gang is The Professor, a small man with a large round head which contains a great criminal brain. He knows nothing about cricket and so mugs it up by reading *The Principles of Sound Batmanship* by L. E. G. Glance. He tries out his new-found knowledge on cricket-loving strangers by inserting into the conversation phrases like 'Long live Sir Sutcliffe', or 'What sweeter music than the crack of the willow despatching the leather to the ropes across the green tapis.' His two assistants are a gum-chewing Damon Runyan character called Sawn-off Carlo, big, burly and a gangster of the lowest type, and Ralph the Disappointment, who was sacked from his public school for drinking port and later joined the Foreign Legion.

So much for the baddies, and already I suspect you will have discerned Mr Alington's great gift for creating character. The goodies are based at the village of Wattlecombe Ducis in Glebeshire, the home of Sir Timothy Blood – 'erect, distinguished, with a noble white moustache, the Doyen of the game'. He is the father of England's captain, Norman Blood, 'dark, handsome and an athlete to his finger-prints'. Another villager is Joe Prestwick, a spin bowler for Glebeshire and tipped to play for England at the Oval Test. But his parents are 'rough peasants' who 'live in Stark Cottage and wring a bare living from the soil'. As a result poor Joe cannot afford a belt and has to play in his braces, when suddenly called on to play against Baghurst Parva, because the blacksmith has been kicked by a horse. Joe takes all ten wickets for one run, and Monica, the daughter of the saintly and scholarly old vicar, who loves him, buys him a belt. Joe falls in love with her too, and the saintly old vicar interrupts his reading of the 1907 *Wisden* to give his blessing to their marriage, provided Joe plays for England. . .

And there I must leave you in suspense. I hope I have whetted your appetite. How and when will the gang strike? Will the vicar allow Joe to marry Monica? Does England win? Is the British Empire disrupted? All I can say is 'Read on'. I am sure that you – like me – will find it the funniest cricket book you have ever read – and also the most lovable, with its gentle digs at all and sundry in the cricket world.

Brian Johnston, London 1983

Contents

○

THE CRIME IS HATCHED—3

CRICKET-LOVERS ALL—27

PROCEEDINGS OF A SUPER-CRIMINAL—55

THE PROPOSAL—71

THE EVE OF THE MATCH—87

PLAN A—103

WEEK-END TENSION—129

PLAN B—153

EXTRACT FROM THE DIARY OF SAWN-OFF
CARLO—171

ESCAPE—181

PLAN C—195

AFTERMATH—215

WEDDING BELLS—237

EXTRACT FROM THE DIARY OF SAWN-OFF
CARLO—245

" The Bad Men—no information obtainable."

From the dossiers of half the police-headquarters
in Europe

THE CRIME IS HATCHED

" THE Big Shot is late," said Sawn-off Carlo.

" He will come," replied Ralph the Disappointment.

" Sure he'll come, buddy. The Big Guy knows his onions."

The situation of the café, outside which the two men sat, cannot be more closely described than by saying that it was in foreign parts. So much, indeed, was obvious, since local colour of a peculiarly foreign brand surrounded it upon all sides.

It was a scene such as Mr. N. Julius Guggenheim, the famous novelist, has so often described. Brilliant blue sea, about which costly motor-boats with aristocratic occupants dashed and roared. Dazzling white terrace with orange trees and palms luxuriantly flourishing at suitable intervals. A dazzling white town climbing upwards away from the sea, and as a background, distant snow-capped mountains.

Upon the terrace strolled a brilliantly attired throng composed of foreign noblemen, film-stars, adventuresses, financiers, spies of both sexes, secret service men, ambassadors, and international crooks. Snatches of miscellaneous conversation floated about in the dazzling sunlit air, as they strolled to and fro.

" But consider, *mon cher duc*, to abduct the Minister of Foreign Affairs will cost money——"

" *Alors*, my dear Lola, I give you three more days in which to secure the documents——"

" Her Supreme Highness will be wearing the pearls at the *bal masqué* tomorrow night——"

Mingling with the conversations came the strains of a band in dashing uniforms, playing the latest operetta.

The two men sitting at the little round table before the café presented a strange contrast. They were alike only in that they were both members of a gang for whom the police of half Europe were searching, the gang that was bitterly spoken of, whenever detectives came together, as the Bad Men. Already this gang had to its credit the assassination of the President of Guamelia and the blowing up of the National Bank of Gloritana, as well as a host of other major crimes. Always conspicuously upon the scene of the crime it left its signature, " The Bad Men ", scrawled in sprawling red

4

letters. Nothing, however, was known of its members. Police dossiers all over Europe remained tantalizingly empty. Only it was realized and generally admitted that the brain behind this organization was of a subtlety and brilliance quite unprecedented in the annals of crime. It belonged, in short, to that rare being, a super-criminal.

Sawn-off Carlo, big, burly, a round soft hat on his head, his jaws moving continuously as he chewed gum, was a gangster of the lowest type, such as may be seen in many films of American life. He wore a gun strapped under each arm, though this was not so much because he needed them, as because he would have felt undressed without them. He watched the patrolling crowd with little interest. They seemed to him on the whole a phoney lot of palookas. These foreign burgs sure got a guy down. His was a simple enthusiastic nature and he thought often of his old mother who dwelt up a great many stairs in a bum apoitment-house way back in New Yoick.

His companion was English. It would be a pleasure to say that he was English to the backbone, but such, alas, was not the case. He was, in fact, as was indicated by the name by

5

which he was known in many low quarters of the world, a renegade Englishman. Though born in the highest circles and educated at impeccable schools, Ralph the Disappointment had drifted steadily downward. His was a story of steadily increasing shame. He had been expelled from a first-class preparatory school because the Headmaster (who was a snob) had overheard him teasing a Marquis about his boils. He had been expelled from the great public school of Harborough as the result of a far more desperate escapade. It was Ralph's custom to climb out of his dormitory at night and drink port wine in a neighbouring public-house. One night he was surprised in this enterprise by the French master. Without a second's hesitation Ralph shot the man down. Youthful psychology was not understood in those days and a serious view was taken of the offence. The murder of the French master was hushed up (modern languages were never considered of much account at Harborough), but the consumption of alcohol was too grave an offence to be overlooked. Ralph quitted the school in shame. His stern old father, heart-broken at the stigma which had come to smirch the family

name, decreed that the boy must go abroad.
His adoring mother, who lacked her husband's
iron character, protested,

" But if Ralph goes abroad what will become
of him ? He will only drift lower and lower."

" Naturally," replied her husband, voicing
the stern yet simple creed of his class. " That
is what foreign parts are for."

His mother's prediction had come true.
Ralph the Disappointment sank like a stone.
At one time he joined the Foreign Legion, but
here again he was a failure. It is significant
that his companions did not call him Beau
Ralph, as they would have done if he had
been an Englishman of the right type, abroad
in error. On the contrary they spoke of him
cynically as " Ralph the Disappointment ".

It was Sergeant Renee Parbleu, that brutal
bully who thought nothing of kicking an un-
popular legionary to death, who threw this
bitter name at him one day in the heart of
the torrid desert. " *Regardez, mes amis*," he
had cried with a savage sneer, " Ralph the
Disappointment ! "

Immediately the name had stuck ; it was
repeated continuously in a variety of languages. It was strange, Ralph had thought,

how this mixed collection of legionaries could recognize at sight a pukka fella, who had been falsely accused of something at home and would ultimately after incredible hardships be welcomed back with honour. They knew that he was not a pukka fella, but on the contrary a real bad fella, indeed a shockin' fella. Even here amid this vast expanse of sand the stigma lay upon him.

Ultimately he had deserted from the Legion and continued on the downward path, meeting on his way with a number of discreditable adventures, which would fill volumes. And now here he was, a member of the dreaded Bad Men. Even his adoring mother could not have predicted anything quite so deplorable.

The two men sat mainly in silence waiting.

" Say, buddy," said Sawn-off Carlo presently, in order to pass the time, " do I ever tell you how I put Al Camponoli on the spot ? "

" Several times."

" Aw, shucks, that's tough. I guess it's nice woik the way I get that guy's aged mother sorrowing for her son. Do I tell you how I croak Theodore the Gink ? "

" Yes."

Sawn-off Carlo sank into disappointed silence.

8

He was a gregarious soul ; nothing delighted him more than these simple reminiscences of a happy past. He was damped by Ralph's lack of response. Say, did that guy give you the dead pan or did he ?

Presently the man they awaited was to be seen making his way through the crowd towards them. Even at a distance it was clear that here was no ordinary personality. He was a man of small stature, but upon his little body was perched a huge head with an immense dome-like forehead. Beneath it piercing eyes which looked on the world through great round spectacles. He was dressed like any other member of the crowd in white ducks and a yachting cap, but some strange magnetic force seemed to set him apart. In his hand he carried an attaché case.

" Here," said Sawn-off Carlo, " comes the Big Guy."

The approaching man, known to his subordinates as the Professor, was, it may be said at once, the leader for whom the police of half the world were searching. Nor were they wrong in attributing to him intellectual powers of an abnormal kind. A short summary of his career may not be out of place.

He had been born of peasant stock in a humble foreign village. At an extravagantly early age, however, he had shown his mettle. He had begun to speak long before the normal time, and his speech from the first was not as that of other children. For instead of the usual and eagerly anticipated references to his parents the infant Professor had opened his tiny mouth and uttered the startling syllables, " Square Root." For a while after that he remained silent. When next, some weeks later, he spoke again, it was to utter his first complete sentence.

" Parallel lines," he observed, removing his tiny thumb from his mouth, " though indefinitely prolonged, will never meet."

Having thus spoken, he replaced his thumb in his mouth and lying back in his humble cot, relapsed once more into his childish thoughts.

Again at the age of three the Professor showed a further glimpse of his phenomenal intellectual grasp. A certain aunt of his, who was visiting his parents, fancied that she had a way with children. It was this good woman's custom to lean over the cot, with murmurs of " Tootsy-wootsy, babykins " and similar ejaculations. It was an embarrassing moment for

all concerned when the infant Professor remarked coldly,

" Please remove this woman with her absurd
conversation. She is setting up inhibitions
which will be with me through life."

It must be noted that at the time of this
incident the Professor had not yet learned to
read, and could not possibly have heard of
Dr. Freud.

A career of the utmost honour was naturally
predicted for this extraordinary child. And
indeed, the earlier part of his life was brilliantly spent in academic surroundings. Schol-
astic honours of all kinds, the most exalted
academic posts were his for the asking. Many
works of the most startling profundity bore his
name. But alas, the Professor with his phenomenal intellect found the companionship of
even the most erudite and brilliant of his
colleagues lacking in entertainment. It was
he, who, after a five-hour chat with Einstein
upon various mathematical topics, came away
with the memorable words :

" The man is shallow."

The climax came with the completion of
his final work, *The Essence of the Absolute*.
This had taken him four years of immense

concentration, and when finished was found to be both unintelligible and unprintable. For the first time the Professor's mighty intellect had soared into the realms of pure knowledge. With something akin to despair he realized that, however long he lived, he could never know more than he did now.

Suddenly academic haunts knew the Professor no more. No-one knew what had become of him, but to the general relief of his colleagues, who found his superhuman abilities extremely tiresome, he disappeared. No-one, of course, suspected that like Moriarty before him he had become an enemy of society, that he had at last found a congenial outlet for his phenomenal intellect in directing the activities of the Bad Men.

As he approached the table where the others sat, the Professor greeted them with every sign of astonishment. For among his other capabilities the man was a superb actor.

" My dear sirs ! This is indeed a surprise."

" Howdy, Boss," replied Sawn-off Carlo amiably.

" You fool!" whispered the Professor savagely. " Have I not told you that we are to meet always as strangers ? "

" Aw, Boss, there ain't no G-men around in this bum burg."

The Professor fixed upon him a terrible glance.

" It is better, my dear Carlo, to be a Bad Man than a dead man."

With these words, uttered in a tone of appalling menace, the Professor seated himself at the table, and clapped his hands for the waiter. He ordered himself a *café fine* and lit a thin cigar. While waiting for it to be brought, he conversed loudly with his companions, at the same time shooting keen glances about him through his spectacles.

" One of the delights of foreign travel, my dear friends, is the possibility of chance meetings such as this. Here was I, strolling at leisure through this fashionable resort, little dreaming that I was about to encounter my two old friends . . ."

Thus the three sat, to all seeming an innocent enough group of old friends. But when his coffee had been brought, the Professor suddenly dropped his loud and somewhat hearty tone. Leaning forward he spoke quietly and precisely.

" And now, my friends, we speak of business. You know why we are here ? "

" Sure," replied Sawn-off Carlo, " we're going to muscle in on this ball-game racket."

"You are as usual inaccurate," said the Professor coldly. " In England, which is to be the scene of our operations, these contests are spoken of not as the ball-game, but as Matches of Crickets."

Ralph the Disappointment, renegade Englishman though he was, could not help wincing slightly at the Professor's mistake. He said nothing, however. The Professor continued.

" The operations upon which we are about to embark are, I think I may say, of a more far-reaching character than anything we have yet attempted. I flatter myself that though I have already assassinated a President——"

" Say, Boss," protested Sawn-off Carlo, " who is it gives that sap the well-known stream of lead ? "

The Professor waved his cigar impatiently.

" The actual assassination may have been your handiwork. The elaborate and carefully prepared plans, which made it possible, were, of course, mine."

Carlo sighed in happy reminiscence.

" Say, does that punk holler when I give him the woiks ? Oh boy."

14

" Pray," said the Professor coldly, " let me have no more interruptions. As I say, the operations before us are of the most far-reaching importance. They have as their object no less than a blow at the heart of that Empire of which our friend Ralph here is an unworthy member."

Again Ralph the Disappointment winced, but did not interrupt.

" Who our employers are," the Professor proceeded, " must remain a secret even from you, my friends. Let it suffice to say that International Interests of the first importance are involved. In consulting me these gentlemen have shown wisdom of a high order."

" You sure loathe and despise yourself, Boss," said Sawn-off Carlo.

" I trust," the Professor replied coldly, " that I have a tolerably just appreciation of my own remarkable powers. They are, however, not the subject under discussion at the present moment. To return, as the French say, to our muttons. As I have said, the object of our present operations is no less than the complete disruption of the British Empire, a task, which as you can imagine, would probably daunt an intellect less remarkable than mine. Having given the matter some thought, however, and having received reports from a certain trustworthy agent in London, I have been able to devise a scheme of unparalleled subtlety and effectiveness."

Having reached this point the Professor paused and sipped his coffee, while his companions remained in suspense.

" It became obvious to me," he continued presently, " after studying my reports, that the British Empire is held together entirely by a series of contests of this curious Crickets. These contests take place periodically between what is called the mother country and the natives of the various outlying dominions. They are known as Test Matches. Of these Test Matches, none are regarded as of such outstanding importance as those which take place periodically between England and the dominion of Imperia. Am I right, friend Ralph ? "

Ralph nodded without speaking.

" They sound loopy to me," remarked Sawn-off Carlo.

" The English are naturally mad," replied the Professor. " That goes without saying." He opened his attaché case and took from it a thick bundle of type-written sheets. " I have here a series of notes and observations, made by an acute and reliable agent. I will read them to you."

He sipped his coffee again and began to read in a dry, precise voice.

" It is almost impossible to realize, my dear Professor, the extraordinary reverence with which Crickets is regarded in England, not only by what is called in the Press the Sporting Fraternity, but by all classes from the highest to the lowest. When an important contest is in progress—and frequently these mimic battles endure for several days at a time—the arena is always crowded, and onlookers may be heard encouraging the participants with such cries as ' Long live Sir Sutcliffe ! ', ' Leg before, my hat ! ' or ' Sockem, Patsyboy ! ' (this last a technical shout of some kind, whose exact significance I have never been able to discover).

" So firm is the hold which this Crickets has upon Englishmen of all classes, that it has in fact become a synonym for Virtue. Thus an outraged husband discovering his best friend in the embraces of his wife will exclaim, ' This behaviour is not crickets, by Jove,'—a truth, my dear Professor, which would appear to be self-evident. In the course of my researches

17

which have been deep and prolonged, I have only been able to discover one cricketer who was not also regarded as a Pattern of the Highest Virtue. This was a certain A. J. Raffles, who in his non-sporting moments pursued the calling of a burglar. So strongly rooted in the national character, however, is this veneration of Crickets that A. J. Raffles has always been acclaimed as a hero, whereas criminals who do not share his sporting proclivities are universally execrated."

The Professor laid down his notes and regarded his companions through his spectacles.

" And so, you see, my friends, a blow struck at this national custom is a blow at the very heart of proud Albion. Let the natives of Imperia defeat the mother country and her prestige is gone. It will be our duty to see that the mother country is defeated. It shall be done, moreover, in a manner that will lead the English to suspect Imperia of foul play. Thus the Matches of Crickets will cease to be played and the Empire will fall to pieces."

Ralph the Disappointment spoke in a low voice.

" How are you going to do this thing ? "

The Professor smiled.

" As a preliminary, my dear Ralph, we shall hamstring the horses of the Englishmen."

" Gee," exclaimed Sawn-off Carlo, " it's dough for nix, Boss."

" Simplicity, my dear Carlo, was ever the hall-mark of genius."

" Cricket," said Ralph the Disappointment, still in a low voice, " is not played upon horses."

" You are in error, Ralph," replied the Professor, taking from his case another sheaf of notes. " I have here an extensive report upon English Sporting Life in all its branches. Listen. ' The game is played between two teams chosen from the aristocracy and upper classes, who, mounted upon horses, ride hither and thither waving long poles and simultaneously exclaiming, " Chukka and Tiffin ! " These shouts must not be confused with the somewhat similar equestrian exclamations (Yoicks, Tallyho, etc.) which are emitted while in pursuit of the fox.' "

" That is polo."

" What, my good Ralph, is polo ? "

" The game you've been reading about."

The Professor frowned and consulted his notes.

" It would appear that you are right," he said at last. " I was not unnaturally confused by the multiplicity of athletic contests prevalent in England. The matter, however, is of small importance."

" Say," interrupted Sawn-off Carlo, " ain't there goin' to be no hoises ? "

" There will be, as you say, no horses. I shall, however, be able without difficulty to devise some alternative plan."

" Say, Boss, how would it be we take them cricketing palookas for a ride ? "

" A little crude, my dear Carlo."

" I ain't shot up a guy in weeks," pleaded Sawn-off Carlo wistfully.

The Professor muttered impatiently and turned once more to his notes.

" Here is what my agent has to say upon the subject of Crickets. ' The game of Crickets takes place between two teams of eleven men, suitably arrayed in costumes of white flannel. The regulations are of extreme complexity and can only be comprehended in their entirety by the English who begin to study them in earliest infancy.' We need not, however, consider these absurd regulations just now. I flatter myself that what it takes an Englishman a lifetime to understand I shall assimilate within a few hours. The important point is this." The Professor leaned forward and behind his spectacles shone the light of genius, contemplating supreme achievement. " The natives of Imperia are even now upon a visit to England. Four of these Test Matches have already taken place without result. The final culminating contest is to take place in a month's time at a centre of English sporting life known as the Oval. It is there, my friends, that we must strike and strike hard."

At this point there occurred an unexpected interruption. With a sudden harsh cry Ralph the Disappointment sprang to his feet. He began to speak and his voice was choked with emotion.

" No," he cried, " no. I cannot be a party to this thing."

The Professor, his cigar poised, regarded him coldly.

" Rebellion, Ralph ? " he asked in a soft voice, which held infinite menace. The man was always most dangerous when he spoke softly.

Ralph answered wildly,

" Heaven knows I am not a pukka fella, in

fact I am a really bad fella. Mine has been a life full of shame. But there are limits beyond which even the worst fella cannot go. I was ready to join in assassinating the President of Guamelia and in blowing up the National Bank of Gloritana. But to interfere with a cricket match and in particular a Test Match —no, Professor, low as I have sunk, I am not as loathsome as that."

The Professor had listened to this outburst in silence. Now he spoke, and still his tone was one of dreadful softness.

" Look at me, Ralph."

There followed a strange battle of wills. And yet it was hardly a battle. What chance had Ralph, weakened by years of dissipation, against the mighty indomitable will of the man whose eyes bored into his? It was the old story of the rabbit helpless before the boa-constrictor. With a low moan Ralph the Disappointment sank back into his seat, like a man hypnotized.

" So," said the Professor slowly. " You will obey my orders ? "

" I will obey your orders," Ralph repeated, " even though I become a really filthy fella."

" It is well, my friend," said the Professor.

" You shall have your complete instructions, both of you, within a few days. For the moment I have no more to say."

He arose, picked up his case, and bowing from the waist, said in the loud voice, which he had adopted at the beginning of the conversation,

" Good day, my old friends. It is, indeed, a pleasure to have revived these happy memories."

" So long, Boss," replied Sawn-off Carlo. " I'll be seeing you."

The Professor walked away. The others sat on at the table watching the small figure as it made its way through the crowd of spies, financiers, and others. As he went, the Professor's lofty brow was furrowed in tremendous concentration beneath the yachting cap, and he hummed softly to himself, a sure sign that the great brain was at work.

*   *   *

" Gee," said Sawn-off Carlo, " it's tough about them hoises, brother."

There came no answer from Ralph the Disappointment. Glancing at him sideways, Sawn-off Carlo was astonished to see that his companion sat with his head in his hands, his whole being shaken with sobs.

Who knows what bitter memories stirred in the mind of that poor besmirched outcast, as he sat here in this café in foreign parts, confronted with the crowning ignominy of his life —memories of his own first little bat, of happy study of the first-class averages in far-off innocent days ? Life can be very cruel.

W.G.
It is easy to see
Was accustomed to wear
Great masses of hair.
Cricketers, however, of a later day
Refuse altogether to clutter up their faces with
beards in this ridiculous way.

From *Wisden's Almanac Designed to be
read as Literature*

CRICKET-LOVERS ALL

THERE is no need to describe in detail the immense wave of enthusiasm which swept the country during the visit of the Imperian team. It might be—and frequently was—described as unprecedented. From the very moment when, led by Lethbridge their captain, that maker of mammoth scores, they set foot upon these shores, their doings were followed with passionate interest. Their chances and abilities were everywhere discussed. Was this new fast bowler Bumper as great as the fast bowlers of a past day, was the illustrious Lethbridge himself, despite his countless records, the peer of departed giants? Could eleven men be found in all England to withstand the might of Imperia? Lethbridge himself was a silent man. On his arrival he contented himself with observing, " Everyone is very fit ". When questioned about the prospects of the Test Matches he said simply, " May the best team win "—a sentiment which was reciprocated by Norman Blood, the Glebeshire captain, who was ultimately chosen to lead the English eleven at a midnight meeting of the Selection Committee, convened in a cellar in the north of Scotland.

No need to describe the series of grim struggles which took place, without any decision being reached, at Nottingham, Lords, Manchester and Leeds. Worthier pens have already accomplished the task. Never, indeed, have so many writers of the first calibre been engaged to describe a series of sporting events. Not only famous cricketers and journalists but eminent novelists were retained for the purpose at enormous expense. Much startling literature resulted. Mr. Beetling Grim's description of Old Trafford in the rain was generally considered a masterpiece of sombre and ruthless description, as powerful as anything in his celebrated *Stinking Splendour*. Miss Felicia Portcullis (authoress of *Her Chap*, *Misty Eyes*, *A Rich Man's Secretary*, etc.) was, on the other hand, a writer who was never very good at weather, and reached her greatest heights in her description of Norman Blood's century at Lords.

" With a ripple of his bronzed boyish shoulders," so wrote that enthusiastic and prolific woman, " Blood swings his bat. Away flashes the ball, away, away! Instantly pandemonium breaks loose, for Blood has reached his century. A hundred runs for England, you readers. Our Norman. Strong men bite their lips to keep their emotion in check. We, their weaker sisters, frankly shed tears of delight. Lords Cricket Ground rings with happy plaudits. And amidst it all our hero stands leaning gracefully upon his bat, just six foot of clean English thew and sinew. We shall not be there to hear it, of course, but some motherly instinct deep down in the heart of me whispers that when Blood returns to receive the full-throated congratulations of his fellow-cricketers he will say modestly, ' It is for England, you chaps, and after all it's nothing to what Drake did.' Heroes, you know, are like that."

A description of every ball bowled was broadcast to Imperia, and in England the accounts of the play by John Beltravers were listened to raptly all over the country. Business, it might be said, came practically to a standstill everywhere, as the well-known voice related ball by ball the chances and changes of the game. Listeners everywhere shared his emotions at the great first-wicket stand achieved by England's opening batsmen, Hugh and Crigh, at Leeds, at the downfall of the mighty Lethbridge at Trent Bridge, when he had scored a bare seventeen runs.

Letters on all subjects connected with the Test Matches filled the Press to the exclusion of every other topic. Should they be played to a finish ? Should Norman Blood have declared earlier at Lords ? Should the players wear numbers on their backs, so that they might be distinguished by the crowd ? This last suggestion, it may be said, drew from Sir Timothy Blood, father of the English captain and doyen of English cricket, the characteristic retort, " I would rather see the entire English eleven dead at my feet than see them with numbers on their backs."

So the country was engrossed in the one great topic. Gardeners named their newest blooms after the Imperian captain, society women scented themselves with the new Perfume Lethbridge, almost all boys born that year were named after him. It is no exaggeration to say that all England waited with passionate eagerness for the final match to be played at the Oval. For this was to be

played to a finish and would decide the fate
of the Ashes.

*   *   *

And if all England was agog, it may safely
be said that in no corner of it was interest so
high as in the little village of Wattlecombe
Ducis which nestled serenely in the Glebeshire
downs. For it was in the Manor House upon
the outskirts of the village that young Norman
Blood, England's captain, hero of the Lords
match, had been born and bred. Upon its
smooth lawns, in the shadow of its immemorial
trees, he had played beneath his father's tuition
his first faltering infant strokes.

Let us take a glance within those historic
precincts. Upon a certain Sunday afternoon
—exactly a week before the Selection Committee were to meet in a balloon, which was
to ascend over the English Channel, to choose
the men who would represent England at the
Oval—Norman and Sir Timothy paced the
lawn beneath the great immemorial trees.
Father and son presented a distinguished and
highly coloured picture. Norman, young,
dark, handsome, an athlete to his finger-tips,

31

was wearing the vividly striped blazer of the
Glebeshire Globetrotters, tie of the Old Har-
burians and a straw hat surrounded by the
colours of the Strolling Sportsmen ; Sir Timothy, erect, distinguished, with a noble white
moustache, which in its blacker days had been
the admiration of cricket grounds all over the
country, was attired in the blazer of the Wild
Woodpeckers, an M.C.C. tie and a panama
with the same ribbon. Sir Timothy, as has
already been said, was generally regarded as
the doyen of the game. His pronunciamentos
upon all subjects connected with it were eagerly
awaited. It was he who had said at a general
meeting of the Glebeshire C.C.,

" I pray every morning and night that the
captain of England may always be a man of
irreproachable lineage."

And again,

" I shall maintain with my last breath that
umpires should be men of sound conservative
views."

Sentiments which had won the applause not
only of all Glebeshire, but of all England.

As they strolled this Sunday afternoon, Sir
Timothy was in reminiscent mood.

" At Lords," he said, " which as you know,

my boy, is the Headquarters of the game as well as the Mecca of cricket-lovers in all corners of the globe——"

" I know, Father," Norman replied.

And indeed he did, for from his earliest days he never remembered hearing Sir Timothy mention Lords without introducing this noble qualifying phrase.

" At Lords," proceeded Sir Timothy, " and by George, my boy, I love every stick and stone, every brick and blade of the old place——"

" I know, Father," said Norman again.

" At Lords in the Gentlemen and Players match of '97 I was batting with Tiddles Marshbanks——"

" S. P. Q. Marshbanks," put in Norman reverently. " Cambridge and Southshire."

" The same, my boy. I was one of the few who were privileged to address him as Tiddles. Other pseudonyms by which he went were ' The popular ex-Cantab ', ' the celebrated Southshire crack ' and ' the Chevalier of the Straight Bat '. Well, as I say, we were batting. It was, I remember, a lovely day. Jupiter Pluvius, as we old cricketers call rain, was conspicuous by its absence, while Old Sol, which as a result of your education, you will

33

have no difficulty in translating for yourself, shone brightly.   Both of us seemed set for a good score.   But Cricket, which as you know, my dear boy, is the King of Games and the Game of Kings——"

" Amen."

" —is full of surprises.   And that day there were certainly surprises.   Crocker (F.) was bowling from the pavilion end——"

Sir Timothy's anecdote, however, remained unfinished.   For just then a new figure appeared from the direction of the house, that of a young girl.   This was Monica, the Vicar's daughter, who dwelt alone with her saintly and scholarly old father at the Vicarage.   She was an old playmate of Norman's ; indeed, as a child with golden ringlets she had shared in those early games of cricket, during which Norman had laid the foundations of the skill which was to serve England so nobly.   Sometimes they still laughed together over the memory of the donkey-drops, which Monica had been wont to bowl and which often enough had resulted in the shattering of the youthful Norman's wicket.   Many a time when the efforts of the butler, the two gardeners and the chauffeur had failed to dislodge the " young

master " Monica with her artless girlish donkey-drops had succeeded.

Today Monica presented a picture of radiant
young womanhood. Not only was she extremely beautiful, but glowing health seemed
to inform her every movement. Needless to
say, she was adored by young and old in the
village of Wattlecombe Ducis, being often com-
pared by the inhabitants to a ray of sunshine.
The Girl Guides, of whom she was the moving
spirit, all prayed that they might grow up to be
just like Miss Monica ; aged villagers, to whom
she brought small comforts, declared, in the
accustomed manner of aged villagers when
presented with small comforts, that "the sight
of Vicar's lass did them a power of good ". As
she approached she swung a tennis racquet,
which she had lightly caught up when leaving
the Vicarage. She had not been playing tennis, but she was the kind of girl who liked
swinging things.

"Cheerioh, you two men-things ! " she called
gaily as she approached.

The two men greeted her, and Sir Timothy
inquired what she had been doing.

" I've been up at Farmer Clutterbuck's," she
answered smiling, " sitting by a sick cow."

35

" How good you are," said Norman, " and how unselfish ! "

Monica laughed unaffectedly, and gave her racquet a tremendous swing.

" I like to bring gladness wherever I go. Of course it was no good reading aloud to the cow, but I sat beside it reminding it that it was an English cow and must keep a stiff upper lip. The poor animal understood me, I'm sure. It mooed once or twice just as though it were promising to keep steady and not lose its nerve."

" Everyone and everything in Wattlecombe Ducis loves our Monica," said Sir Timothy heartily. " How is your father, my dear ? "

Monica smiled roguishly.

" Poor dear, he is in disgrace. He has been dreadfully absent-minded again. In giving out the second lesson this morning, he said the Epistle to the Imperians, instead of the Galatians."

" Did he, by Gad ? "

" Old Simkins, the verger, has been scolding him dreadfully."

" Well, well," said Sir Timothy. " A stupid mistake, but not altogether unnatural. Though, of course, there are wide differences. The Galatians, for example, were not cricketers."

"But we must remember," said Monica, who, though radiant, was a just girl, "that Cricket had not then been invented."

"True," replied Sir Timothy, and was silent for a moment contemplating the remarkable phenomenon of a cricketless world. "It seems extraordinary that nobody thought of it. I mean to say I can't think what the beggars did with themselves."

"I suppose," suggested Monica, "that they had some games of their own. Ancient sort of games."

"I suppose so," agreed Sir Timothy doubtfully. "It doesn't seem natural though."

Just then a stately butler came from the house followed by a footman. They laid tea in the shade of the great trees and withdrew.

"Ah, the tea interval," exclaimed Sir Timothy jovially. "Monica, my dear, you must pour out for us."

The three formed a charming group as they sat about the tea-table in the shadow of the immemorial trees, Sir Timothy's elderly and highly coloured dignity contrasting with the youthful vitality of the other two. It was not often that a woman's presence graced the Manor tea-table, for Lady Blood had passed

37

away almost unnoticed during the University match of 1927. It was a mellow picture such as could occur only in a corner of rustic England. Through the immemorial trees shone Old Sol.

More than once, as they ate cucumber sandwiches and sipped tea, Norman's eyes rested upon the slim girlish form of Monica. How strange, he thought, that the gay child of the golden ringlets, who had bowled donkey-drops with such devastating effect should develop into this beautiful young woman ! Quite often recently he had wondered whether he should not invite her to become mistress of the Old Manor. He felt that she would grace it worthily. Certainly she was tremendously radiant, but then the Manor was a large house, and after a while you would not notice it. Sometime, when the all-important match at the Oval was over and the Cricket Season finished, he must give the matter serious consideration. . . .

From time to time he caught Monica's eye and smiled. She blushed slightly and looked away.

" Did I ever tell you youngsters," said Sir Timothy presently, drawing a cigar from his case, " how I scored twenty-five in one over from Slogger Jameson in the Middlesex match of '94 ? We were playing at Lords, which as you know, Monica, my dear, is the Mecca of cricket-lovers all over the world . . ."

*   *   *

Remarkable as it may seem, Norman Blood was not the only inhabitant of Wattlecombe Ducis whose name was illustrious in the cricket world. For in that doubly blessed hamlet dwelt also Prestwick (J.) the young Glebeshire spin-bowler, whom pundits were tipping as a possibility for the match at the Oval on the strength of a remarkable performance against Wessex only last week. Seven good Wessex wickets had Prestwick taken for a meagre twenty-four runs, bringing his total bag for the season up to one hundred and nineteen. If he did well in the Westshire match which was now in progress, his inclusion at the Oval seemed almost certain.

Prestwick's rise to fame had been one of the sensations of the present season. It was only last year that had occurred that memorable day when Prestwick played first for the village of

Wattlecombe Ducis. The occasion was the match against Boghurst Parva, always regarded as a "needle" match by the inhabitants of Wattlecombe Ducis. The rival teams were already assembled round the pavilion, the two captains were about to toss for innings, when word came that Tom Apps, the blacksmith, Wattlecombe's demon bowler, had had an accident with a horse he was shoeing and could take no part in the match. Consternation reigned. To take the field without Tom Apps spelled certain disaster ; more particularly as among the stalwarts of Boghurst Parva was observed a young gentleman actually wearing a Harlequin cap. Rumour went swiftly round that this was a friend of the Vicar of Boghurst Parva's eldest son, a batsman of the highest order.

Something, however, had to be done and Providence in its inscrutable fashion ordained that young Joe Prestwick should be standing by the Pavilion about to watch the game. To him spoke Bill Sniper, the Wattlecombe Ducis captain,

"Ever played cricket ? "

"Only once or twice."

"You've got to play now. Come on."

So hurriedly was it all arranged that, Boghurst Parva having won the toss, Joe Prestwick most regrettably had taken the field wearing braces.

The opening phase of the game more than confirmed the pessimistic feelings of Wattlecombe Ducis. The young gentleman in the Harlequin cap proceeded to score freely off the depleted bowling, while his partner, Bill Wicks, the Boghurst Parva grocer, stolidly kept up his end. At the end of half an hour the scoreboard read :

40

o

o

In despair the Wattlecombe Ducis captain looked round his men. All his regular bowlers and others had tried and failed. At last he inquired of Joe,

" Can you bowl ? "

" I can try," replied the youth who was to become famous as Prestwick (J.).

They still talk of that day in Wattlecombe Ducis. Joe tossed his first ball into the air ; the young gentleman in the Harlequin cap smiled contemptuously. And then a shout went up from the assembled spectators. The young gentleman's off-stump was seen to be leaning backwards.

When he got back to the pavilion, he explained angrily,

" His braces put me off. You can't expect a fellow to bat against a man in braces."

But before long his colleagues knew that he was lying. Within half an hour the entire Boghurst Parva team was back in the pavilion for a meagre total of forty-seven. Joe had taken ten wickets for one run.

Monica, of course, was watching the match. It was she who, mounting her bicycle, bore the news to Sir Timothy at the Manor.

" Sir Timothy, Sir Timothy, come quickly. They have discovered a demon bowler."

Sir Timothy, calling for his car, reached the ground in time to see Joe take the last Boghurst Parva wicket.

" But, good heavens, child," he exclaimed, " the fellow is playing in braces."

Monica was excited and momentarily off her balance.

" Does it matter ? " she asked.

" I would rather," said Sir Timothy in his outspoken way, " see the whole village dead at my feet than a man bowling for the team in braces."

Monica said nothing. Of course, Sir Timothy was right . . . In her first girlish enthusiasm she had allowed herself to be blinded to the real and important things of life. Suddenly she was inspired. Mounting her bicycle, she rode rapidly into the village, not dismounting until she reached a haberdasher's shop.

" I want please," she said breathlessly, " a gentleman's cricketing belt."

" Yes, Miss. Did you fancy any particular shade ? "

" It doesn't matter. Only hurry."

Within a few minutes she was back at the ground. Joe, who was more astonished than anyone else by what had happened, stood about watching the efforts of the Wattlecombe Ducis batsmen. He stood alone, for although he had taken ten wickets for one run, no-one cared to be seen with him while he still wore his shameful costume.

Suddenly a feminine voice beside him said,

" Wear this, please."

Turning, he beheld the most radiant girl he had ever seen, holding in her hand a cricket belt. So overcome was he that at first he did not recognize the Vicar's daughter. She seemed to him a goddess from Heaven. He contrived to stammer,

" Thanks, awfully."

" Not at all," she answered correctly, and then her impulsiveness gaining the upper hand once more, added, " Wear it, please, for my sake. Good luck ! "

And that was all. But it was enough for Joe. He had fallen in love above his station.

Joe was no batsman, but inspired by Monica's presence, he compiled two not out. The Wattlecombe Ducis total reached sixty-four, and in the second innings Joe bowled the entire Boghurst Parva team out for twelve runs.

As the last wicket fell, Monica approached Sir Timothy.

" Well, Sir Timothy, isn't he good ? "

" Trousers," replied Sir Timothy grudgingly, " should be kept in position by invisible means or failing that by a scarf bearing the colours of a good club. But," he added, his sense of justice coming to his rescue, " the boy is undoubtedly a discovery."

After that memorable day progress was rapid. Joe was tried for the Glebeshire 2nd XI and repeated his success. Towards the end of the season he was tried for the county itself. In the following year, that of the Imperian visit, he became a regular member of the team, earning the dark blue cap of Glebeshire with its crest of a scarlet dragon. More than one fine achievement he had to his name, and once he had been awarded by a well-known firm a cake for the outstanding sporting feat of the week. And now he was spoken of as a " possible " for the great match at the Oval.

All England knew of Joe's sudden rise. But what all England did not know was that Joe still kept the belt which Monica had given him, and gazed at it often in rapturous adoration. No knight ever preserved his lady's favour with greater enthusiasm. Since that day of the Boghurst Parva match he had loved Monica with all the ardour of his simple athlete's nature. The home of the Prestwicks was very different from the Manor house, for Joe's parents were but rough peasants, who wrung a living from the soil. It was in the little attic where he slept that he kept his belt hidden away. It was a red and white belt with a snake-shaped buckle, which it was Joe's pride to keep clean and shining. Often he would take it out and look at it, and though he still reddened with shame, as he thought of how he had taken the field wearing braces, the belt brought him thoughts of Monica and what she had done for him that day.

In his simple adoring way he had studied the habits of his beloved. It was not by chance that he and Monica so often met in the village. This evening, for instance, being Sunday, she would, he knew, walk to church. And so it happened that while Monica, having finished tea at the Manor House, walked gracefully back to the village, Joe was waiting to meet her.

He waited upon the village green. Here was a scene of much natural beauty, which could easily be described at great length and with much erudition. But for our present purposes it is sufficient to say that Wattlecombe Ducis was a delightfully old-world village, and that picturesque cottages and suitable vegetation were present in generous quantities. The Earthy Peasant, the old-world village inn, was not yet open and the green was almost deserted. Joe's thoughts, as he loitered, ran upon Monica, his Lady of the Cricketing Belt, as he sometimes poetically called her in his own mind. How lovely she was! He

46

began as he stood there to compose a poem
in his own mind.

> " *O Monica, whose lovely face,*
>   *Is matched by thy tremendous grace.*"

Suddenly he started and blushed violently.
She was coming. Monica was coming. He
watched her approach gracefully round the
village pond, still swinging her tennis racquet.
He heard her call out in her radiant fashion to
the ducks,

" Cheerioh, you old ducks ! "

Small wonder that all Wattlecombe Ducis
adored her.

To describe the conversation which followed
in all its beauty and tensity would require the
pen of a Felicia Portcullis. Indeed that excellent and best-selling woman has in most of
her novels described very similar scenes. Perhaps the nearest is that in *A Rich Man's Secretary*,
in which a certain Frank Greatbatch " felt his
whole virile being flooded with tenderness at
the womanly fragility " of the lady he was ultimately to marry. Emotions upon this terrific
scale took hold of Joe, as he watched Monica
approach. Suppressing them, however, in
manly style he raised his hat.

" Good evening, Miss Monica."

" Hullo, old Joe."

She struck him as she spoke a light welcoming blow with the tennis racquet. Within her, too, emotions of the Felicia Portcullis order were aroused by the meeting. For it must now be disclosed that Monica, though above him in social standing, returned Joe's love with an ardour equal to his own. That very first day when she had handed him the belt, her woman's intuition had pierced beneath the shame of his costume and glimpsed the simple nobility beneath. She yearned now in her girlish way to bring gladness into Joe's life.

A long silence followed the greeting since Joe was struck speechless by her beauty, and remained with his eyes bashfully fixed upon the ground. At last he spoke.

" Are you going to Church ? "

" Yes, I've been having tea at the Manor."

At this a series of sensations which Felicia Portcullis has aptly called " the searing torments of the green-eyed monster " attacked the luckless Joe. Norman Blood was his captain and the best amateur bat in the country, but it was heartbreaking to think of his wealth and all that he could give Monica, whereas he himself . . . This reminded Joe of his own gift to Monica, and he said shyly,

" There's something I'd like to give you, Miss Monica."

The tennis racquet wobbled in her grasp.

" A present for me ? "

" Yes. It's not much, I know. It's not like the presents a rich man could give you, but I'd like you to have it."

He felt in his pocket and produced a cigarette card, which displayed a highly coloured version of his own features and beneath it his name. Joe, greatly daring, had added the words " With love ", so that the whole read " With love from Prestwick (Glebeshire) ".

Monica's eyes glowed as she took the present.

" Thank you, Joe. Oh, it's top-hole."

" They're giving them away with packets of Red Queen," he explained. " It's got the story of my life on the back."

" I shall always value it," replied Monica simply.

They walked on in silence towards the church.

" Only a week now," said Monica presently, " until the team for the Oval is chosen. Oh, Joe, I hope you play."

" The Selection Committee," Joe loyally replied, " is above reproach."

" Oh, of course. All the same it would be wonderful."

" Thank you, Miss Monica."

She turned towards him and said softly,

" Won't you call me Monica ? "

Joe started and rich colour flooded his face.
" May I ? "

This was a great moment in his life. Never had he aspired to such intimacy. Various speeches formed in his mind—" Monica, darling, I am only a pro, playing his first season for the county——" " Dear Monica, I may be of lowly birth——" But he bit them all back. How could he, modest village lad that he was, aspire to win the hand of this radiant girl ? All the same, he knew well that before long the time would come when he must speak.

They came presently to the little village church. And here, with a tremendous handclasp on Monica's part, they parted.

" Good night, old Joe."

" Good night, Monica."

Monica, having left her tennis racquet in the porch, went into the church. It says much for the stability of her character that she was able to keep her mind upon the service. Not many girls, having received amorous glances from two first-class cricketers upon one day, would have been able to do so, but Monica was made of stern stuff.

Joe, meanwhile, walked slowly home. His thoughts were mixed. Although the memory of her presence still made him dizzy, he could not help thinking sadly of Norman Blood and all the wonderful presents he would be able to make her. Jewels, tiaras . . .

He was still lost in these thoughts when he reached Stark Cottage, the lowly, almost derelict home, where he dwelled with his rude old parents. His rude old mother, standing at the door, greeted him.

" Thou bëest läte, läd."

The older Prestwicks, it must be confessed at once, were not peasants of the jolly " hey-nonny-no ", " green-grow-the-rushes-oh " type. On the contrary, they wrung a bare living from the soil and behaved accordingly. They conversed always in the manner which is called racy of the soil ; that is to say with two dots over almost every word.

Joe stooped to kiss his mother's rude old cheek and passed into the simple squalor of the cottage. In the rough kitchen sat his father, smoking a filthy clay pipe and spitting frequently, as men do when they wring a living from the soil. A sheep lay asleep on the hearth-rug.

" 'E mün bör gürt wür dönee," snarled Mr. Prestwick senior, at the same time aiming a brutal kick at the recumbent sheep.

Joe did not answer, but pursued his way upstairs to his attic.

" I love my old parents, of course," he reflected, as he went, " but what a pity that wringing a bare living from the soil makes people so terribly rude ! "

" It is a solemn thought that if I had been born in the underworld, I might have been the most sensational criminal in the country instead of just the most sensational dean."

Dean Crunch at the Annual Gala of " The Old Lag's Uplift Association "

PROCEEDINGS OF A SUPER-CRIMINAL

None of his fellow-passengers patrolling the deck of the cross-channel boat that summer afternoon, ten days before the great Oval Test Match, realized that there was anything unusual about the seemingly inconspicuous little man with the lofty, dome-like forehead, who sat by himself, smoking a thin cigar. Those who troubled to consider him set him down as possibly a harmless University don, returning from a holiday abroad. Certainly none of them guessed that here was a man, upon whom half the police in Europe would have liked to lay their hands, a man who was destined within a very short while to convulse an Empire to the very roots of its being.

The Professor was deeply engrossed in a book. And it was typical of his Napoleonic care for detail that the book which he perused was *Principles of Sound Batsmanship*, by L. E. G. Glance, with twenty-five action photographs. He had begun to read the book in the train from Paris, and so great was his intellectual grasp that he felt himself already master of this complex and difficult subject.

Nothing, as the steamer ploughed its way onward, disturbed his tremendous concentration. Only for a moment, when the white cliffs of Folkestone first came into view, did he raise his eyes and gaze through his spectacles at that distant prospect, while his lips twitched in a sardonic smile. Then he returned to his studies.

" The off-drive," he read, " of which the late S. P. Q. Marshbanks (Cambridge and Southshire) was perhaps the greatest exponent (see plate seven) . . ."

He read on . . .

His plans were now practically complete, for it was his custom to reach decisions with lightning rapidity. As in the case of the assassination of the President of Guamelia, the blowing up of the National Bank of Gloritana and his other major achievements, he preferred to mature his schemes in solitude. To Ralph the Disappointment he had already given certain vital secret instructions, but not until the last moment would he impart to his subordinates the exact nature of his plans and their own part in them. Before he left for England he had arranged for the three to meet, as though by accident, at The Panatrope Music Hall in London. Before then he had certain highly important preparations to make.

Folkestone. Amid the bustle and confusion of arrival, the Professor, still inconspicuous, descended the gangway.

He found himself presently in the train heading for London. He was seated in a smoking compartment, which he shared with two men, a stoutish prosperous-looking man, who sat in the far corner and a tall man with a thin moustache, who sat opposite the Professor. Upon the platform at Folkestone a newsboy had been shouting, " Latest Cricket Scores." Each of the Professor's neighbours had bought a paper and become instantly immersed.

" Evidently," mused the Professor, " I have had the good fortune to encounter at the outset two members of the Sporting Fraternity. Here is an opportunity to test my knowledge, acquired from the admirable L. E. G. Glance."

The opportunity occurred shortly. The man with the moustache looked up from his paper and ejaculated,

" Cor, Blood out for six."

The Professor, seizing this chance to break
through the celebrated English reserve, leaned
forward and addressed him.

" You are interested, my friend, in
crickets ? "

The member of the Sporting Fraternity
started slightly, but admitted,

" Ar, that's right."

" I too," said the Professor, " though I have
never wielded the willow, am a devotee of the
National Pastime. As L. E. G. Glance has
observed in the preliminary pages of his noble
work *Principles of Sound Batsmanship*, ' What
sweeter music than the crack of the bat,
despatching the leather to the ropes across the
green *tapis* ? ' "

" Go on," said the member of the Sporting
Fraternity cautiously.

The Professor, taking this as an invitation to
proceed, did so.

" The off drive, of which the late S. P. Q.
Marshbanks (Cambridge and Southshire) was
possibly the greatest exponent, has always
seemed to me a particularly noble stroke.   Do
you not agree ? "

" That's right," said his neighbour.   At this
point, English reserve set in again and he

returned to his newspaper. It was not long, however, before a second startling piece of news led him to exclaim, " Cor, old Lethbridge has got another century."

" Ah, yes," said the Professor. " One of the natives, I think. Indeed, if my memory is not at fault, the outstanding native."

" Cor," went on the man with the moustache, " he's a treat, that boy. I grant you he's not cultured, not classical, but can he adopt the long handle ? "

It was now the Professor's turn to be cautious.

" No doubt," he said. " Probably the longest of handles."

" Cor, yes. Look at Lords. If it hadn't been for old Lethbridge at Lords——" He leaned forward and with the air of one imparting a vital and confidential piece of information, added, " If you ask me, old Blood ought to have declared earlier at Lords."

" Declared what ? " asked the Professor unguardedly and realized instantly that he had made a mistake. The member of the Sporting Fraternity was staring at him with an air of the greatest surprise and distrust. The Professor recovered himself quickly.

" Excuse my humour, by Jove," he said gaily. " I am one that can never resist a jest."

He realized, however, that he had lost the confidence of the member of the Sporting Fraternity. With a slightly bewildered murmur of " Ar, that's right," the man returned to his paper.

At this point, the stout gentleman joined in, addressing the man with the moustache.

" If you ask me, do you know who is the boy we want at the Oval ? "

" No."

" Young Prestwick."

" Ar."

" He mixes 'em, young Prestwick does. I saw him bowl against Gritshire in June. Give him the kind of wicket he wants and he'd run right through the Imperians."

" Ar, that's right."

" Funny to think that only last season that boy was playing for the Second XI. If I was on the Selection Committee——"

In this vein the two members of the Sporting Fraternity continued all the way to London. The Professor, leaning back in his corner, permitted himself to smile ironically. Let England array all her heroes ; they would avail her nothing.   A single small man with a giant's brain would defeat them all. . . .

★   ★   ★

It is impossible to follow too closely the movements of the Professor upon his arrival in London.   Let it suffice to say that he proceeded with that mixture of audacity and caution which had always been one of his most striking characteristics, and which served to keep police-dossiers all over the world empty concerning him.   His astonishing faculty for disguise and his amazing powers of impersonation also stood him in good stead.

Upon a certain morning, for example, he might have been observed, carefully attired in sporting costume, grey bowler, check suit, field-glasses slung about him, upon his way to the Oval.   He had always regarded it as of the first importance that the terrain should be carefully studied beforehand.   Before the assassination of the President he had spent many hours in the Guamelian presidential dwelling, disguised as a member of the staff.   Moreover, he was anxious to see for himself this crickets which appeared to loom so large in the national life of England.

A contest, he found on his arrival, was in progress—a match, indeed, between the Clergy of the South and the Clergy of the North—but he was amazed to find the vast arena practically deserted.

" Can it be," he thought, " that I have been deceived about the national enthusiasm for crickets ? Or is this an indication of religious decay in England ? In any case it is very strange. Since, however, I am here, I will make such observations as I can."

He sat down upon a seat of concrete and unslinging his glasses surveyed the scene. The contest proceeded in a suitably religious silence ; the flannelled priests ran about with the utmost enthusiasm, though there were no spectators to cheer them. From time to time the Professor called aloud, " Long live Sir Sutcliffe ! " " Chukka and Tiffin ! " and " Sockem Patsyboy ! ", but it seemed that his efforts at encouragement met with little response. One priest, indeed, who was stationed close to where he sat was observed to start wildly at these strange cries issuing from the solitary spectator. Presently, the Professor abandoned his pose of enthusiastic sportsman ; his great brain began once again to formulate his plans. Here upon the scene of his forthcoming operations he checked every detail and could find no flaw. Plan A, Plan B, Plan C . . .

There was another day, when his small figure was to be seen in a part of England very far removed from London, in the streets of a small market town in the heart of Loamshire. For the purpose of this expedition he was impenetrably disguised as an artist. The great dome-like brow was concealed beneath a wide-brimmed black hat ; he wore a big floppy bow tie, and a black velvet jacket ; with consummate attention to detail he carried an easel under his left arm.

He halted presently before the premises of Messrs. Axley and Clutterbuck, the house-agents. After lingering a moment to read the advertisements displayed in the window he entered.

A clerk rose to greet him.

" Good morning," began the pseudo-artist. " Are you Axley or Clutterbuck ? "

" Actually neither."

" Ah, well, it is of no importance." The pseudo-artist deposited his easel and seated

himself. " Listen, house-agent, I am the celebrated Popplewick, R.A., of whom you have
doubtless heard. I am, as you are possibly
aware, particularly famous for my painting of
moorland scenes. My ' Evening on the Moors '
which hangs now in the Tate Gallery is a case
in point. Or again my ' Morning on the
Moors " which was recently purchased by the
Fulchester Art Gallery, instantly springs to the
mind."

" Yes, but——"

" Do not interrupt me, house-agent. I am
now approaching the point of my visit. I have
long intended to paint the sweeping expanses
of scenery to be found in this neighbourhood.
With this object in view I propose to settle here
for a short while. In short, house-agent, as
you say in your admirable profession, I desire a
res."

" How many rooms ? "

" It is not of the slightest importance."

" Oh, but, I say——"

" The only condition upon which I insist is
that the res. must be sit. in surroundings of the
greatest loneliness. For one of my temperament and artistic eminence seclusion is impera-
tive. I should prefer, too, a res. with a cellar,

with a strong door.   Many of my canvasses are of immense value."

Before he returned to London upon the following day the spurious Popplewick, R.A., had become the tenant of an old deserted stone house in the very heart of the Loamshire moors.

Finally there was an evening when the Professor might have been observed traversing one of the lowest thoroughfares of the city.   It was a street of evil repute from which even the police shuddered and hurried away as quickly as possible.   But the Professor entering it displayed no sign of fear.   He was disguised with masterly thoroughness as a rough character, and as he walked he sang the roughest song in the English language which he knew would be well in keeping with his disguise.   From mean dwellings upon either side the inhabitants regarded him with menacing looks.   But the Professor was not daunted.

" Blimey, by Jove," he called out, adopting a rough accent, at the same time drawing his forefinger across his nose in a vulgar fashion, to indicate that he was one of the lowest of the low.   The watchers assumed that he was a rough character like themselves and let him pass unmolested.

He came at last to what was probably the vilest haunt in the street. Halting before the door he knocked three times. At last a glimmer of light showed and the door was cautiously opened by a hunchback Chinaman of repulsive aspect.

Evidently the Professor was expected, for the Chinaman said at once,

" You wishee speakee Flash Alice ? "

" At once, please," said the Professor, momentarily dropping his impersonation of a rough character.

The Chinaman stood aside and he passed in.

Half an hour later he emerged, and, after a cautious glance up and down the street, set off on his return journey. As he neared the corner a policeman appeared. In a flash, the Professor, adopting his rough accent, called out,

" 'Struth, old copper."

" Merely one of the criminal classes indulging in rough persiflage," reflected the unsuspecting policeman.

Little did he realize that the greatest criminal of the age had just addressed him !

★   ★   ★

An hour or so later, as the Professor removed the last traces of his disguise, he smiled to himself with a certain complacence. His preparations were complete. Nothing for him to do now but await the meeting at the Panatrope Music Hall.

" But only God can make a really effective spin-bowler."

Song

THE PROPOSAL

"T'ÖLD söw be main gürt sick, sö 'er be, dönee," observed Mr. Prestwick senior.

The family sat at supper in the squalid kitchen of Stark Cottage. Rough food was distributed on rough plates. Mr. Prestwick had been wringing a bare living from the soil all day ; great hunks of it still clung to him and sweat glistened on all the visible parts of his person. Just now he was worrying a bone ; great knotted veins stood out all over him, as he chewed and growled. Mrs. Prestwick, though not perspiring to quite the same extent as her husband, presented a typical picture of a rude peasant's equally rude wife. She sat, for example, with her elbows on the table.

Joe, sitting between them in his neat dark suit, made a strange contrast. He sat silent throughout the meal, though this was not because he despised his rude old parents, but because he knew that he was faced with a crisis, the greatest crisis, indeed, of his young life.

71

He knew that the time had come when he must speak to Monica.

The Westshire match was just over, Glebeshire having won by a narrow margin. But very nearly they had not won and Joe was fully conscious that, had they been defeated, the fault would have been largely his. During the Westshire second innings he had been fielding at long-leg. A lengthy stand by two of the Westshire men was in progress, and Joe most reprehensibly had allowed his thoughts to wander. He had begun to think about Monica. Indeed, he had begun to try and conclude the poem, the opening lines of which had come into his head upon the evening he gave her the cigarette card.

> " *O, Monica, whose lovely face*
> *Is matched by thy tremendous grace——*"

So far the poem proceeded smoothly and without difficulty. It was the next couplet that teased and worried poor Joe. He tried,

> " *I'd rather wed thee, Parson's daughter,*
> *Than bowl out Lethbridge with a snorter.*"

But he was not altogether satisfied. He tried again,

> " *I'd rather wed thee, dear, you ken,*
> *Than get Lethbridge l.b.w. (n.)* "

No, that was not good enough either.

> " *I'd rather wed thee, lovely maid——*"

Then he gave it up and thought about Monica, how lovely she was, and how unworthy he was of her, and fixed his eyes bashfully on the ground. It was then that disaster happened. Swiggins, the Westshire batsman, receiving a full-pitch outside the leg-stump, hit the ball to long-leg, a high swirling catch. Joe, his eyes fixed bashfully on the ground, did not observe it. A warning cry from his captain told him of the ball's approach. Too late he perceived it dropping towards him out of the cloudless sky. Too late he made a desperate clutch. But without avail. The ball fell to the ground. From the supporters of Glebeshire arose a derisive groan.

Trembling with remorse and shame Joe threw in the ball. He felt in his deep humiliation that he could not face the stern questioning eyes of Norman Blood, nor the silent reproaches of his colleagues.

Next day the press had recorded his shame.

" At this point Swiggins enjoyed a stroke of

luck, being missed at long-leg by Prestwick. The chance was one that should certainly have been accepted."

Neither of his parents could read, and so fortunately need never know of their son's disgrace, but Joe tasted the depths of bitterness, as he thought of Monica reading those shameful words. He knew that the crisis had come. He must speak to Monica at once and ask her if she could ever love him. If she could not, then he must just bite his lip and try to forget. But he must know. This suspense was interfering with his cricket.

And so he had written her a note.

" DEAR MONICA,

" I must see you tonight. Can you meet me by the seat on the village green at nine o'clock? I have a very important question to ask you.

" Yours faithfully,
" J. PRESTWICK."

The time was now nearing nine o'clock. With a muttered word of apology Joe rose from the table and went out.

" Häppen," remarked Mrs. Prestwick, " läad be goin' cöurtin'."

" Eh? Döst think thät, Möther? "

" Häppen," replied Mrs. Prestwick cautiously.

" Eh," proceeded Mr. Prestwick after a long pause, during which he drew his great knotted arm across his mouth, and filled his filthy old pipe, " but I be main pöwerful feared."

" Aböut läad, Fäther ? "

" Näy, Möther, aböut t'öld söw. Faïr main gürt sick, sö 'ër be dönee."

After this interchange the senior Prestwicks rose from the table and prepared to spend an evening of bestial sloth.

Joe, meanwhile, after a quick, loving look at the belt, left Stark Cottage and walked towards the village green. It was a lovely evening. Behind the Earthy Peasant the sun was sinking, a fiery red disc, just, thought Joe in one of his poetical flashes, like a gigantic new cricket ball. He came to the green and sat down upon the seat to wait. The sun sank lower, painting the westward sky with a mass of fiery tints. Was it coincidence, wondered Joe, or was it a favourable omen that Nature in her grandeur should reproduce almost exactly the colours of the Glebeshire Globetrotters ? As the minutes passed he could no longer sit still. The suspense was worse than waiting to go in number eleven, as he always did, during a close finish.

Presently he saw her approaching. He watched her walk gracefully round the pond. She was wearing a simple girlish white frock and was swinging a golf club which she had lightly caught up on leaving the Vicarage. His heart bounded.

She drew near. He stood up and raised his cap.

" Good evening, old Joe."

" Good evening, Monica."

They sat down upon the seat. Joe was seized with shyness and remained silent.

"You said in your note," she prompted him at last, " that you wanted to ask me a question."

" It's true." For another long minute Joe wrestled with himself. Then he took the plunge. He said in a low voice, " Monica, yesterday I missed a catch."

" I know," she answered gently, " I read of it in the paper."

" The paper said that it was a chance that should have been accepted. It's true. It should have been accepted."

" Then why," asked Monica artlessly, " did you not accept it ? "

Joe bowed his head.

" I was thinking of something else."

She was not the kind of girl to spare even those she loved.

" That was very wrong, Joe."

" I know, I know," he answered wildly. " Don't think I haven't tasted the bitterest remorse. But I could not help myself." He was silent for a moment and then faltered, " I was making up a poem. A love-poem, Monica."

" Oh, Joe ! When you were fielding at long-leg ! "

" Don't reproach me, Monica. I know I deserve it, but I just couldn't help it. Would you like to hear the poem ? "

" Oh, yes."

Staring at the façade of the Earthy Peasant behind which the sunset had now almost faded, Joe began to recite,

> " *O, Monica, whose lovely face*
> *Is matched by thy tremendous grace*——"

Beside him he heard Monica gasp.

" Oh, Joe ! You mean you missed a catch because of me ? "

77

" Yes," he answered boldly. " That's why I had to speak to you tonight. The thought of you is spoiling my fielding. Monica, my darling, I'm only a cricket pro——"

" Only ! " she exclaimed in a thrilling voice.

" But I love you, Monica. I've loved you ever since that day you bought me a belt. Do you remember ? "

" The day you won the match for Wattle-combe Ducis."

" But in my boyish ignorance I played in braces. Until you saved me from shame. That was like you, Monica. So tender always, so thoughtful for others. Oh, Monica, will you marry me ? "

There, he had spoken now. What would she answer ? Would she be angry ? Would she think him presumptuous even to have aspired to her hand ? He could scarcely believe it when he heard her sweet voice reply,

" Here, Joe, is a chance that will certainly be accepted."

" You mean you will marry me ? "

" If Father consents, Joe."

" Oh, Monica darling, I can hardly believe it." And then in his elation a sobering thought occurred. He said slowly, " Are you sure you don't mind my parents being only rude old peasants ? "

" As though I could ! " she answered. " Besides, I don't suppose they are as rude as all that."

" I'm afraid they are," he said sadly. " They are a bit gnarled too. It comes of wringing a bare living from the soil. Are you sure you don't mind ? "

" Gnarled or not," cried Monica proudly, " they are the parents of the man I love."

They walked back presently to the Vicarage, for Monica was impatient to ask the Vicar's consent at once. When they reached the door, she said,

" Wait here, Joe. I will go in and ask Father."

The saintly old Vicar was in the library, a *Wisden's Almanac* for 1907 open upon his knee. Monica ran to him and fell on her knees beside him, her eyes glowing.

" Father, I have wonderful news——"

The saintly old Vicar looked up from his reading.

" Just a moment, my dear. I was just studying the score of the Harborough and Egby match of 1907. I remember that well. It was

79

the year my straw-hat was cleaned. R. J. Trump not out two. A dreadful snick through the slips that was." For a moment the old man was silent, his eyes far away, as though he gazed upon scenes long past. Then with an effort he returned to the present. " Well, now, my child, what is this exciting news ? "

" Didn't you ever guess, Father, that a day would come when I should bring you the most wonderful news of all ? Mr. Right has come along, Father."

" Would that," said the saintly old Vicar, " be R. T. Wright, who played for Cambridge in 1902 ? "

" No, no, Father, you don't understand. I am in love. I want to be married."

"But, my dear," her father protested, " R. T. Wright must be quite an elderly man by now. He was certainly an admirable bat in his day, if a little uncertain in the field, but I don't see how you can possibly marry him."

" Father, Father, please listen——"

In a few eager words she told him all. The Vicar shook his snowy head doubtfully.

" Young Joe Prestwick is undoubtedly a first-rate spin-bowler, but he lacks social advantages. His parents are very rude."

She flashed back,

" Joe is one of Nature's gentlemen."

" Ah, my dear, but that does not entitle him to use the Gentleman's Entrance of Life. I had always hoped that one day you would marry young Norman Blood."

" I am very fond of Norman, Father. But I love Joe."

" Well, my child," the old man answered, " I hardly know what to say. This is a great shock to me. Young Joe comes of peasant stock. The elder Prestwicks, to be candid, are but little removed from the beasts."

" But some beasts," argued Monica, " are gentle and quite human in their ways."

She thought sadly, as she spoke, of her beloved fox-terrier, Wiggles. How she had adored that dog and loaded him with kindness ! Unfortunately her custom of swinging him lightly by the tail, as she walked, had undermined the beast's nervous system. He had begun to bite people in the village quite recklessly, and had been found a new home.

" Besides," she added, " Joe may play for England at the Oval."

The old man's face softened.

" In that case, my child, I dare not refuse."

" Oh, thank you, Father. May I bring in Joe and tell him ? "

A moment later Joe was in the library.

" Joe," cried Monica, " Father says we may be married if you play for England at the Oval."

Joe replied in manly style,

" I could wish for nothing better, sir. We are in the hands of the Selection Committee."

" Yes, my boy," replied the saintly old Vicar, and added reverently, " May Providence guide them rightly in their decisions ! "

" Oh, Father," cried Monica, " that means that you want me to marry Joe ? "

" No," replied the Vicar, " I am thinking of the supreme importance of beating Imperia."

" Amen," said Joe.

*   *   *

Later that night, when Joe had gone home, Monica stood alone at her bedroom window. She was swinging her toothbrush which she had lightly caught up on leaving the bathroom.

Her thoughts were all with her beloved Joe. He must play at the Oval. He must. She thought of his strength and his manliness and of his googly which no batsman could ever detect until too late.   Looking forward into the future she saw herself as the perfect cricket professional's wife.   She saw herself bringing gladness into the lives of the Glebeshire eleven, she saw herself upon the county ground watching her man bowl—even her adoring heart could not shirk the fact that Joe's batting was of a primitive kind—she saw herself at home in the long domestic evenings, oiling his bats, working out his average with loving care, teaching his children, perhaps, the first simple rudiments of bowling.

Oh, Joe must play at the Oval !   He must !

Up in a balloon, boys, up in a balloon,
Choosing the English team, while sailing round
the moon.

Song of the Selection Committee

THE EVE OF THE MATCH

DAYS of suspense followed, during which all England held its breath. A kind of hush of expectancy seemed to brood over the country. One question occupied all minds. Who would be the thirteen men chosen by the Selection Committee from whom the final eleven would be picked ? Would Frank Manleigh, the fast bowler, be given another chance or would he be displaced by Plugg of Downshire ? Would Prestwick be chosen, as well as or in place of Truth, that veteran of twenty Test Matches who had hitherto been England's favoured spin-bowler ? Would young Gayheart of Wessex be given another chance ? Everywhere these burning questions were discussed ; every day the Press was full of letters from those who advocated their favourites. The form of likely players was eagerly watched. Glebeshire supporters were overjoyed when Joe advanced his claims by taking five wickets against Gritshire, the champions. The doings of the Imperians were also closely watched ; the whole nation shuddered when on Wednesday Lethbridge scored 427 not out in two hours against Dudshire.

Much was written too in the Press upon the subject of Timeless Tests, and Mr. R. B. Parsley, the famous dramatist, caused much confusion by an article in which he explained that there could be no such thing as a Timeless Test, since all the Test Matches that had ever been played were still being played as well as all the Test Matches which were as yet in the womb of time. This was felt to make the whole subject much more difficult and to have complicated the work of the Selection Committee to an unnecessary degree, since if Mr. Parsley were right they might just as well choose W. G. and Ranji and make quite sure of beating Imperia.

So all England waited, and no-one, it can be readily understood, waited more impatiently than Monica, for though she was patriotic to the core and placed England's honour above everything, she was, as Miss Felicia Portcullis has remarked in her great political romance *Susie O' the Left Wing* or *Clean of Heart though a Communist*, " a woman above all and her girlish heart cried out for Love of her Man." It was difficult for her, as she went about her humble tasks in the village, gladdening the lives of those about her, swinging various objects that came handy, to think of anything but the match at the Oval and Joe's chances of playing. Suffering villagers found her, though sympathetic and radiant as usual, oddly absent-minded.

Suspense ended at last. Very late upon Saturday night the Selection Committee ascended in their balloon. When, their deliberations concluded, they descended in time for the names of the chosen to appear in the stop-press columns of the Sunday papers, it was discovered that the thirteenth and final name was that of Prestwick (Glebeshire).

Monica rushed to tell her saintly old father the glad news.

" He's chosen, Father. Joe is chosen. Here is the list of names."

The Vicar scanned the list, carefully.

" That is a very interesting selection," he said at last, " but, of course, Prestwick may not play. He may be twelfth man, or even," he added as an afterthought, " thirteenth man."

That, alas, was true. In her elation Monica had not thought of it. But she said bravely,

" I'm sure he will play, Father. Fate could not be so unkind."

" Well, well, my dear, we must wait and see. Much will depend upon the state of the wicket."

" Oh, Father, I love Joe so dearly."

" Quite, my dear child, quite. But there are more important things in this life than our own personal feelings. There is, for example, the question of getting Lethbridge out twice on an Oval wicket. I suppose it would hardly be in order to pray for rain at today's services. Lethbridge has never been quite at home on a wet wicket."

" Father, I do so want to be married."

" Yes, my dear, I know. By the way, I have discovered that the R. T. Wright we were talking about the other day died in 1927. So you couldn't have married him, anyhow."

Monica felt that she could wait no longer. She must see Joe and talk over the great news with him. She left the Vicarage, swinging the umbrella-stand which in her excitement she had absent-mindedly caught up, and set out in the direction of Stark Cottage. At the same time Joe, having broken the news to his sweaty old parents, who had received it with brutish indifference, set out to visit the Vicarage.

Many times on his way he was stopped by peasants who had heard the news and wished to congratulate him.

" Ee be pröud, läad, räckon," they said in their honest way. For they were all rude countrymen, and spoke with two dots over their vowels, though none were as rude as Joe's parents. The elder Prestwicks were by far the rudest people in Wattlecombe Ducis, probably, in fact, in all Glebeshire.

Joe thanked them all and continued on his way with a full heart.

It was in the old spot by the village green that he met Monica. As he saw her approaching his honest young being was flooded with love. How beautiful, how graceful she looked, carelessly swinging the umbrella stand ! What a mate for a humble village youth, born of rude parents ! By the time they met, he was so overcome that he could hardly speak. It was left to Monica to open the conversation.

" Oh, Joe ! "

" Oh, Monica ! "

" If only you are chosen, Joe ! "

" If only I am chosen, Monica ! "

" Oh, Joe ! "

" Oh, Monica ! "

The two young people stood side-by-side on the green, talking, dreaming . . .[1]

*   *   *

The Panatrope Palace of Varieties. The great auditorium packed, beneath a heavy pall of tobacco smoke. Upon the gaily lit stage the Five Dreary Sisters, the rage of the present season, singing in their own inimitable fashion the song which was just then sweeping all England,

> " *The Warder's son and heir*
> *Lisped his first young baby prayer*
> *In the little old prison underneath the elms.*"

So sang the Five Dreary Sisters clustered about a microphone, and the simple touching words floated out over the auditorium, awed into tense silence. In the third row of the stalls sat the Professor, smoking his inevitable thin cigar and surveying the Five Dreary Sisters through his great round spectacles. He was attired in a dinner jacket, and none of those about him in the stalls guessed that he was anything but a tired business man seeking recrea-

---

[1] These dots have no sinister significance. They merely indicate that the ensuing conversation is too dull and unimportant to be reported at length.

tion. In order to complete the illusion the Professor occasionally murmured aloud in a tired voice such phrases as " invoice " and " overhead charges ". He believed in leaving nothing to chance.

A few rows farther back sat Ralph the Disappointment. His dissipated face wore a haggard and morose expression, but this was due not so much to the moving performance of the Five Dreary Sisters, as to the bitter thoughts which stirred in his mind. He was back now in the land from which years ago he had fled in shame. All about him in the stalls sat his fellow-countrymen, relaxing after a day of honest toil. How these men would shrink from him in repulsion if they could guess the appalling crime upon which he was engaged! And now, not for the first time, he regretted his own mad folly in drinking port while still at a great public school. Men of his own breed would have forgiven him that unfortunate affair of the French master, but the other was unforgivable. Small wonder that in the Foreign Legion no-one had ever thought of calling him Beau Ralph!

In the dress circle Sawn-off Carlo sat and placidly chewed, his round soft hat upon the back of his head. He watched the Five Dreary Sisters without enthusiasm. A dumb set of janes. This London seemed to him a kinda slow burg. Twenty-four hours he had been here, and had not seen a single citizen beaten up or a single bank raided. Say, what did these saps do with their time, anyway? It sure set a guy thinking of his home town, where such simple pleasures as he loved could be had for the asking. Only this afternoon he had visited a cinema to see a film called *Pride of the Homicide Squad*. To sit in the darkness and listen to the homely sounds of a machine-gun and the sirens of police cars had filled him with nostalgia almost too great to be borne.

On the stage the Five Dreary Sisters, clustered about the microphone, still sang :

> " *Little old lags forgot their shame*
> *And learned to play the game*
> *In the little old prison underneath the elms.*
> *Each man after arrest*
> *Came to that cosy nest,*
> *He tried to do his best.*
> *And when the Governor's wife was blessed,*
> *In the little old prison underneath the elms*
> *All loved the infant maid*
> *And the prison organ played*
> *In that little old prison underneath the elms . . .*"

The song ended presently amid thunderous applause. The curtain descended, rose again to display the Five Dreary Sisters smirking and bowing, descended. The interval.

With the final descent of the curtain each of the three Bad Men rose from his seat and joined the stream flowing towards the bars. It was in the Dress Circle Bar that, apparently by the merest accident, the three met for the first time since leaving foreign parts.

On perceiving the others the Professor threw up his arms and exclaimed,

" My George, my old college chums ! "

And so superb was the man's acting that there was no-one in the Dress Circle Bar but thought that here was a chance meeting between old friends.

" Howdy, Boss," said Sawn-off Carlo.

The Professor scowled terribly, but ignoring Sawn-off Carlo continued,

" This is indeed a surprise, by Jove ! Heigho, how long it seems since our mad-cap student days at Oxford University ! "

A look of perplexity dawned on Sawn-off Carlo's good-natured face.

" Say, Boss, I ain't never been a student no place."

95

" Tush, Carlo," the Professor hissed beneath his breath, " you grow more stupid every day."

Sawn-off Carlo obediently fell silent. But he was hurt. The Big Shot sure always got him wrong. Maybe it was his own fault. He wasn't so good at this super-criminal stuff. He was just a great big simple-hearted gangster with an old mother who wept over him in a bum apoitment house way back home.

" We must drink, my old chums," the Professor continued, " to celebrate this happy reunion. Ho there, mine host, three glasses of foaming English ale ! "

When the drinks were brought the Professor led his companions to a quiet corner. But not as yet did he drop his impersonation. He raised his glass, crying,

" Cheerioh, my companions ! A health, as we old students say, to our Alma Mater."

The toast having been drunk, he lowered his voice.

" Well, my friends, our plans are in train. You brought It over safely, Ralph ? "

" Yes." Ralph answered also in a low voice. " It's where we arranged."

" Excellent, excellent. For the moment I

shall say no more. We shall be joined presently by a lady."

" Gee, a doll, huh ? " exclaimed Sawn-off Carlo. " Say, what's the big idea of this frail, Boss ? "

" That will unfold itself. Suffice it for the moment to say that the co-operation of Flash Alice is essential to my plans."

Almost as he finished speaking, there came across the Bar towards them a flamboyantly dressed young woman with hair of flaming red and immense violet eyes. She walked with slow feline grace, one hand resting negligently on her hip. Cheap jewellery blazed all over her. Gee, thought Sawn-off Carlo in his tough simple fashion, has that doll got swell curves or has she ? He guessed she was the kinda dame he could fall for in a big way.

It was easy to see at a glance that Flash Alice was not a splendid radiant girl like Monica. Flash Alice was not, in fact, a splendid girl at all ; on the contrary she was, despite her glamour, Bad all Through. Her downward career resembled that of Ralph the Disappointment in that she had been born of respectable parents, who dwelled in fact in Golders Green. She owed her downfall, however, not to a youthful crime but to the fact that at an early age she had become a Beauty Queen. Seven years ago she had been acclaimed Miss Bogpool-on-Sea, and photographed in her bathing costume standing beside the Mayor. As is well known, early prominence of this nature inevitably gives a girl a taste for champagne, cocktails, jewellery and bad companions generally. And so it was with Flash Alice. Almost immediately she had quitted Golders Green, leaving her respectable parents heartbroken, and started upon her career of shame. Flash Alice's name was never mentioned now in Golders Green ; only that regrettable photograph of her standing beside the Mayor reminded her parents of what might have been.

The Professor welcomed her loudly.

"My hat, my delightful niece ! This is indeed a surprise. Allow me to present to you, my dear, my old college chums."

" 'Evening, boys," said Flash Alice. " Gin and tonic for me."

" Glad to know you, sister," said Sawn-off Carlo. " Sit down, honeybunch."

Ralph the Disappointment greeted her wistfully. He recognized a fellow-outcast when he met one.

" And now, my friends," the Professor spoke with lowered voice, " to our business. I have devised a plan. Or rather I should say three plans. They are, if I may say so without vanity, probably the most subtle and far-reaching plans that even I have ever devised. Let us call them Plan A, Plan B, and Plan C. I will explain to you now Plan A . . ."

For a few minutes he spoke in clear concise terms. So masterly was his exposition, so clear-cut in every detail, that before the Bar began to clear for the second half of the performance his companions understood precisely what was required of them under Plan A.

As soon as the exodus began the Professor gave the signal for the party to break up.

" *Au revoir*, chums of my boyhood ! " he cried for all listeners to hear. " How I have enjoyed reviving the memory of old pranks ! "

" So long, Boss," said Sawn-off Carlo. " Say, honeybunch, I'll be seeing you."

" Certainly not," snapped the Professor. " As soon as Plan A is completed Flash Alice will disappear. That is essential."

" Aw, Boss, that's tough. I guess me and this frail could get together in a big way."

" Listen, Carlo," said the Professor, and his

voice was soft and full of menace, " am I the great brain behind this organization or are you ? "

Carlo grinned amiably.

" Okay, Boss, I guess the dame has gotta disappear."

The party dispersed and returned to their seats. The stage was occupied now by the first turn of the second half of the programme, Les Tuck and his Hot Swing Boys. They were playing another of the popular successes of the day, The Little Old Garage in the Village Square. Into the microphone Mr. Les Tuck's hot boy vocalist crooned the words of the refrain,

> " *Little old angels hovering there*
> *Round the garage in the square*
> *In the evening sweet and calm*
> *Guard the baby cars from harm* . . ."

The great audience listened enraptured.

*   *   *

The days passed ; the date of the great match approached. On the Thursday Lethbridge scored 279 not out against Chalkshire. England sighed and waited.

Where are you going, Cricket fans of England ?
(Oh my Fry and my Hayward long ago !)
  We're going to the Oval, we're going to the
    Test Match.
(Oh my Hobbs and my Sutcliffe long ago !)
  What do you pray for, Cricket fans of England,
  Marching along with your sandwiches and beer?
  We pray for the sunshine, for boundaries and
    overthrows,
  Which, though we can't explain it, always make
    us cheer.
(Oh my Woodfull and my Ponsford long ago !)

Card o' the match, Card o' the match, Card o' the
  match !

  Here's luck to you all then, Cricket fans of Eng-
    land,
  Forming a queue with your sandwiches and
    beer.
  Fate send you sunshine, boundaries and over-
    throws,
  Though why the last excite you was never very
    clear.
(Oh my Brown and my Fingleton long ago !)

Card o' the match, Card o' the match, Card o' the
  match !

  A soft seat all day for threepence.

                                          Ballad

PLAN A

LONG before dawn, that memorable day, the queues began to form outside the Oval. Steadily, as the hours passed the numbers increased, swelling into a great patient multitude. From all parts of London, from all parts of the British Isles they came, these patient lovers of cricket, to witness the great match. A sky of cloudless blue promised a perfect day and a plumb wicket. Surely there must be mighty deeds done that day. Would there be a century from Norman Blood, a great stand by Hugh and Crigh, a dashing display by young Gayheart, a mammoth score by Lethbridge? Who knew? Such things were on the knees of the gods.

Presently the great waiting crowd began to file slowly through the turnstiles. It was then that a somewhat unusual incident took place. A large man, whose jaws worked unceasingly, was heard to inquire of his neighbour,

" Say, is this the right joint for the ball-game, buddy? "

He was taken for a madman and not molested. Thus one more ugly incident was avoided by the traditional good-humour of an English crowd.

As the hour of play approached, the ground was packed. In the more expensive stands men and women famous in the national life were seen to be assembling, for all the world as though this were a fashionable first-night. In the pavilion Sir Timothy was to be seen greeting other veterans only slightly less celebrated, men whose initials have passed into history. Sir Timothy, who was wearing the tie of the Merry Moonrakers, was in optimistic mood.

"We shall beat them," he observed to Q. E. D. (" A wicket an over ") Marjoribanks, who was wearing the tie of the Eastshire Emus. "I have a distinct whathisname that we shall beat them."

Q. E. D. Marjoribanks said that he hoped so, but that in these new-fashioned timeless tests there was no knowing what would happen, and R. S. V. P. Hatstock (tie of Westshire Woodlice) said that with modern bowling and modern wickets it was a wonder any match was ever finished.

In the Press-box were other men with great
names. Old cricketers, both English and
Imperian, gripped their pencils. Twenty-five
of them had already written that Old Sol was
in the ascendant, and seventeen that the wicket
resembled a billiard table. Mr. Beetling Grim
was in his place, though he was in rather a bad
temper because his new novel, *Filthy Luka* (the
story of a Bulgarian dancing girl), had received
an adverse review in the *Saturday Gazette*.
However, he cheered up presently because the
sight of the gas-works gave him an idea for a
new novel altogether. A story of the Gas
Light and Coke Co.—*Within Seven Days*. Stern
old John Therm, ruthless both with his em-
ployees and consumers, refused to admit the
new methods advocated by his son. He
ground his workmen in the dust. Despite
strikes and powerful scenes with his son and
incredible suffering on the part of a number of
minor characters, he went relentlessly on his
way. The whole would end up uproariously
with a terrific explosion which blew thousands
of people to bits, together with the suicide of
old John. Just the kind of thing Mr. Beetling
Grim could do to perfection.

Miss Felicia Portcullis was there, and her,

too, the gas-works inspired with a new theme. *Love's Meter.* Sally Truegirl, misty-eyed and courageous, went as a typist to a branch of the Gas Light and Coke Co. She was very poor and sighed for silk stockings and Life. Cyril Mesurier, the handsome young branch manager, was a rotter where girls were concerned, whereas John Humble, who was merely an honest young workman, was true all through. One evening, when Sally's urge for silk stockings became almost intolerable . . .

In his own little private box John Beltravers waited, John Beltravers, whose voice was to bring to all that part of the population of England which could not be at the Oval the story of this mighty match.

The Prestwick parents could not afford to stop wringing a bare living from the soil for one day ; moreover, they were so rude that they would not have understood what was going on. But Monica and her saintly old father, who had been invited to stay for the duration of the match at the Blood town house in Mayfair, were seated in one of the stands. One thought was uppermost in Monica's mind, as she gazed out over the great green field, and more than once she gave voice to it,

" If only Joe is playing, Father ! "

The saintly old Vicar looked doubtful.

" It is hardly a spin-bowler's wicket, my child. Dear me, I almost wish I had prayed for a little rain. That wicket looks to me just the kind on which Lethbridge might stay in for several days."

Not far from Monica and her father was seated a short figure, with a great dome-like forehead who gazed out over the crowded arena through enormous spectacles. He was attired in the same manner as upon his former visit to the Oval, grey bowler, check suit, glasses slung about him. A typical member of the Sporting Fraternity. It was characteristic of his greatness that he showed no sense of strain at the approach of the climax of his long matured plans. Indeed, a kind of icy detachment appeared to possess him as he smoked his thin cigar, as though he alone among this vast crowd cared nothing for the outcome of the match.

Presently it was seen that Norman Blood and Lethbridge had come out to toss. The news went round that England had won. And shortly afterwards appeared men, bearing boards, on which were written the names of the chosen players. Monica had much ado to bite back her tears, as she read that Joe was twelfth man.

" But I must remember," she told herself, " that it is England that matters. I must just be a splendid English girl and keep a stiff upper lip."

The ground was cleared, bells rang, the umpires appeared. And then punctually at half-past eleven the yellow-capped men of Imperia, led by great Lethbridge, descended the pavilion steps. Photographers rushed to photograph them. In the Press-box thirty-eight journalists simultaneously wrote " a battery of cameras ".

Then came a mighty roar, as England's opening batsmen Hugh and Crigh were seen to emerge and walk towards the wickets. Many in that vast throng must have wondered what the two said to each other during that long walk, so heavy with a sense of destiny. They would, no doubt, have been considerably astonished, if they could have overheard the conversation. For what Hugh said to Crigh was,

" How are you feeling, Bill ? "

And Crigh answered, " Well, it's an extra-ordinary thing, Fred, but I feel sleepy."

" It's an even more extraordinary thing, Bill," rejoined Hugh, " but so do I."

*   *   *

There can be few periods in our national life, so tense, so fraught with solemnity as the opening overs of a Test Match. A great hush, as though Time itself waited upon the unfolding of historic events, lay over the Oval, as Hugh, having taken guard, scanned the disposition of the fieldsmen, patted the pitch, and caused the sight-screen to be moved, prepared to face the first ball. Almost at his feet crouched the four short legs, silly point and three slips who prayed that the ball might snick off the bat into their hands. Bumper, the Imperian shock bowler, began his long run from the Vauxhall end.

Nor was it only to the thousands packed about the Oval that the solemnity of these first moments communicated themselves. All over England, to the teeming millions of great cities, to the lonely shepherd, temporarily ignoring his sheep, went the voice of John Beltravers.

" Bumper is running up. One, two, three, four. Hugh waits, solid, majestic, like a king awaiting the deference of his subjects. Eighteen, nineteen. Bumper is still running. A hostile bowler, this Bumper. Tall, strongly built, full of menace. There is an enormous crowd here today. Men in panama hats, girls in bright dresses. Bumper still running. Forty-four, forty-five. Hugh still waiting like a king. The Imperian fielders in their yellow caps all crouching. Sixty-five, sixty-six. Bumper is nearing the wicket now. He's there. He BOWLS. Outside the off-stump. Hugh moves across, full of majesty, smiles contemptuously and leaves it alone. Bumper starts walking back . . ."

Half an hour passed, an hour, with the tensity undiminished, the solemn hush still unbroken. Once again at twelve-thirty the voice of John Beltravers brought news to waiting England.

" There is no score yet. Hugh not out nought, Crigh not out nought. Total nought. Grim back-to-the-wall stuff, this cricket. Every ball full of drama. The fielders still crouching there full of menace . . ."

As the minutes passed, some thoughtless members of the crowd began to shout derisive encouragement. Once or twice the little man with the dome-like forehead startled those

about him by shouting " Long live Sir Sutcliffe ! " and " Chukka and Tiffin ! " ; but for
the most part the struggle went on in the grim-
mest silence. Time crept on. Twelve-forty-
five. And still no score. In the pavilion, Sir
Timothy could be heard maintaining that in
his day England would have scored at least ten
by now.

And then something did happen, the first
indeed of the series of unusual incidents which
were to make this match one to be long remembered in the annals of Cricket. A fast ball
from Bumper inadvertently struck the edge of
Hugh's bat. The ball trickled between the
slips. No fieldsmen near. Hugh began to run.

The crowd began to applaud the first score
of the match, but the clapping died away when
it was observed that Crigh had toppled gently
over and lay at full length upon the grass.
A gasp of amazement went round the packed
ground. What could this mean ? Imperian
fielders gathered about the prostrate man.
Crigh lay with his eyes closed, and as they bent
over him the bewildered Imperians heard the
sound of a snore.

It was Lethbridge himself who put into words
the idea which had formed in the minds of all.

" He seems," said the great man, " to be asleep."

The umpire bent down and shook him.

" Here, come on, wake up."

No result. The umpire, greatly astonished, turned to confer with his colleague at the other end. Then it was observed that Hugh also lay at full length upon the ground, breathing stertorously.

" Gosh," exclaimed the astonished umpire. " He's asleep now."

In the strange telepathic way that news travels about a cricket ground the tidings reached the pavilion that England's opening batsmen were fast asleep.

In the pavilion Sir Timothy exclaimed indignantly,

" A man can't go to sleep while batting for England. The thing is unheard of."

" It's this new-fangled off-theory and leg-theory," growled R. S. V. P. Hatstock. " I always knew a man would go to sleep one day."

" Nonsense," snapped Q. E. D. Marjoribanks, " it's these timeless tests. I'm dashed if I see how fellows can be expected to keep awake."

" If you ask me," said P. T. O. Brown, " it's this modern craze for averages. Men start doing mental arithmetic at the wicket and this is what happens."

Out in the middle, meanwhile, a hasty conference was held. An excited buzz went round the Oval, as it was seen that the fieldsmen were carrying the unconscious forms of Hugh and Crigh back to the pavilion. There they were laid gently to rest.

" Well, well," exclaimed Sir Timothy, who almost came to believe that his oft-repeated wish had come true and that at any rate a portion of the English team lay dead at his feet, " this is most extraordinary. Most extraordinary."

A stout man in a trilby hat pushed his way forward.

" Let me see these men. I am a doctor."

He bent over the prostrate men, conducted certain tests and presently said,

" As I thought. These men have been drugged."

There was a tense silence. Only Sir Timothy found words to contradict this extraordinary suggestion.

" Nonsense. You can't be a proper doctor.

This is a Test Match. Men aren't drugged while playing for England."

"Modern wickets are often doped," said Q. E. D. Marjoribanks, "but not modern batsmen."

"Get some more doctors," said Sir Timothy.

A second doctor was found who wore an M.C.C. tie, but this obviously more reliable man only confirmed the original diagnosis. Drugged!

Outside the crowd began to clap ironically. They had paid good money to see cricket and were not to be thwarted. The game must go on. With a determined look on his handsome face Norman Blood buckled on his pads and walked to the professionals' dressing-room. Here news of further disaster awaited. Little Teddy Trimmer, England's first wicket batsman, lay curled up in a corner fast asleep.

"What does this mean?" inquired Norman, staring in amazement at the unconscious man.

No-one could enlighten him. Norman, having looked around his bewildered men said finally to little Croxton, the wicket-keeper,

"Feel sleepy?"

"No, Skipper. I feel fine."

" Very well. You and I will hold the fort for England."

A great cheer went up as it was seen that Norman Blood himself was prepared to play a captain's part at this critical moment, a still greater cheer as presently he flicked the ball away for a neat single. First Blood, jested nineteen journalists simultaneously, to England.

Gallantly for the remainder of the morning Norman and little Croxton, the wicket-keeper, battled. At the luncheon interval the score-sheet read :

Hugh, retired drugged	.	.	.	.	o
Crigh, retired drugged	.	.	.	.	o
*N. Blood, not out	.	.	.	.	7
†Croxton, not out	.	.	.	.	1
Extras .	.	.	.	.	o
Total (for o wickets) .	.	.	.	.	8

* Captain
† Wicket-keeper

*　　*　　*

The great crowd surged out over the ground to inspect the wicket and observe the spots where Hugh and Crigh had fallen. Meanwhile the news of the morning's extraordinary happenings went about the country. The lunch-time editions of the evening papers scattered startling news bills. **AMAZING SCENE AT THE OVAL** screamed the *Evening Flagpost*, the *Evening Messenger* had **FOUL PLAY IN TEST** (which was apt to be misunderstood), while the *Evening Planet* in more conservative fashion merely remarked **NEW RECORD AT THE OVAL.** The *Evening Planet* loved records, and here surely, if ever, was an unassailable record ; never before in an international cricket match had both opening batsmen been drugged upon the same day.

In addition to all this the voice of John Beltravers touched upon the affair in his summing up of the morning's play.

" Well, I must say we never expected to see England's opening pair carried off the ground sound asleep. But this cricket is a queer game. You never know quite what is going to happen. There they were being carried off, Hugh just as solid and kingly in his sleep as he is when awake, Crigh, short, dapper, alert, snoring a little, but looking very peaceful. A heavy sleeper, this Crigh . . ."

It had been decided that Scotland Yard must

be informed of what had happened, and during the luncheon interval Steady as a Rock Posse [1] of the Big Six arrived in a police car. The burly bowler-hatted man immediately made his way into the pavilion, followed by a photographer, finger-print expert and others. He was in good spirits, for it was not often that a crime occurred at the Oval during a Test Match. Competition had been strong among the Big Six to be put in charge of the case. Steady as a Rock, however, thanks to his seniority, had won the day ; he was determined if possible to make the case last out until the end of the match.

In a big room in the pavilion, the walls of which were hung with photographs of famous old cricketers, he found Sir Timothy and others surrounding the still prostrate forms of Hugh and Crigh. He shouldered his way through and looked upon the still figures.

" Rigor mortis," he said after a rapid glance, " has obviously set in. How long would you say these men had been dead ? "

" They're not dead," replied the doctor in the M.C.C. tie. " They're drugged."

[1] See *The Vanishing Celebrities*. In this simple and unobtrusive fashion books are often advertised.

Steady as a Rock was not the man to show his mortification. " Drugged ? " he said sternly. " I understood this was a murder case. Well, never mind. I shall unravel it. Get busy, boys."

This last command was addressed to his subordinates, who at once sprang into activity. The photographer took pictures of Hugh and Crigh from every possible angle, the finger-print expert started hunting about for finger-prints.

Steady as a Rock meanwhile took out his notebook, and surveyed the ring about the unconscious batsmen.

" Now then, I want some information."

Sir Timothy pointed to the prostrate forms.

" A foreigner has done this."

" Possibly," agreed R. S. V. P. Hatstock, " though, of course, it might equally well have been a socialist."

" That is true," said Sir Timothy. " I have often said that I would rather see all the pavilions in England burned to the ground than see them containing a foreigner or a socialist. Well, I have been proved right."

Steady as a Rock interrupted, addressing Sir Timothy sternly,

" Who are you ? "

No-one had asked Sir Timothy this question in a cricket pavilion for over fifty years, and he was naturally offended.

" I am Sir Timothy Blood," he answered haughtily, " the popular veteran and doyen of the cricketing world."

Steady as a Rock wrote this down, and then adopting his fieriest cross-examination manner, barked, " Anything to say ? "

" Only that I shall thank Heaven with my last breath that this did not happen at Lords."

Steady as a Rock was on him like a flash.

" Why not at Lords ? "

" Because, my dear fellow, Lords is the Mecca of cricket-lovers all the world over."

Steady as a Rock noted this.

" What is this Mecca, anyway ? " he asked sharply.

Here was another question that no-one had ever asked Sir Timothy. He answered coldly,

" Frankly, I do not know. I have always imagined it to be a very large cricket ground somewhere in Asia. Do you know anything about it, R. S. V. P. ? "

R. S. V. P. Hatstock shook his head.

" Nothing whatever. I expect you're right, Sir Timothy. Do you know, Q. E. D. ? "

Q. E. D. Marjoribanks shook his head. " No idea. But I don't very well see what else it can be."

Steady as a Rock Posse's eye passed from one to the other.

" Who are these other gentlemen ? " he asked.

" These," Sir Timothy replied, " are popular and genial veterans of the cricket field. They are not, however, doyens. I am the only doyen present."

" What is a doyen ? "

" Good heavens ! " exclaimed Sir Timothy angrily. " I never knew anyone ask so many foolish questions. A doyen is an old and very distinguished cricketer with a white moustache. And now for goodness' sake stop fiddling about with that notebook and find out who drugged these unfortunate men."

Just then a burst of clapping from outside indicated that the Imperians were once again taking the field. Steady as a Rock closed his notebook.

" Nothing more can be done until these men recover consciousness. Rest content, gentlemen. The Yard has this case in hand."

Having uttered these heartening words, he went outside to try and find a good seat.

The game proceeded normally after luncheon. It was obvious, however, that the English team were unnerved by their unusual experience of the morning. Their batting seemed to lack confidence. Each man seemed to fear that either he or his partner might suddenly topple over and begin to snore. Consequently, despite a fighting innings of 47 by Norman Blood, the total had reached only 97 for 5 wickets at the tea-interval.

It was during the tea-interval that Hugh stirred and woke. He was evidently under the impression that he was still at the wicket, for, as he stirred, he uttered the single syllable,

" No."

Almost simultaneously Crigh opened his eyes. Instantly he clutched his bat which lay at his side and springing to his feet adopted his stance, as though about to receive the bowling. Then he stared at those surrounding him in dazed fashion and inquired,

" Am I out ? "

" You have been," replied Steady as a Rock Posse, who had been hurriedly summoned, " but you're all right now."

" I don't remember getting out," muttered

Crigh. "Was it that wretched l.b.w.(n.) again ? "

" My brave fellow," said Sir Timothy, " you have been the victim of a dastardly trick. Some villain has attempted to tamper with our national pastime."

" Lor," said Crigh. "Who can it have been ? "

" That," answered Sir Timothy nastily, " is for the police to discover, if they can."

Steady as a Rock proceeded to take charge of the case. He took out his notebook again and addressed himself to Hugh and Crigh.

" Now, you two, have you any idea of how this happened ? "

Neither could offer an explanation.

" You took nothing to drink of any kind before going in to bat ? "

" Only," said Hugh, " the special drink that Mr. Blood sent us."

" I ? " exclaimed Norman. " I sent you no drink."

" But the waitress," persisted Crigh, " told us that you had sent it specially. She said that the drink had special tonic qualities and we were to drink it to the health of England. Isn't that right, Hugh ? "

" That," corroborated Hugh, " is right."

" See here, boys," snapped Steady as a Rock. " What was she like—this waitress ? "

Hugh answered, " She was a very pretty but rather fast-looking girl. She had very red hair and violet eyes. And glamour, lots of glamour."

" Parade all waitresses here instantly," barked Steady as a Rock.

This was done, but among the assembled women was no waitress of the appearance described by Hugh and Crigh. Nor could any of them recall a colleague who could possibly be said to fit the description.

" We're getting somewhere, now," muttered Steady as a Rock. " The drug was in a drink brought by a bogus waitress. I reckon we've got to find that girl with the red hair and violet eyes."

" Why not," suggested Sir Timothy, " find out if there are any foreigners on the ground and if so arrest them ? "

" Or socialists," amended R. S. V. P. Hatstock.

" Or socialists," agreed Sir Timothy.

Just then news was brought that Teddy Trimmer had also regained consciousness.

" Send him in," barked Steady as a Rock.

As soon as the England first-wicket batsman entered, Steady as a Rock shot at him the question,

" Now, Trimmer, you were brought a drink which was purported to have been sent you by Mr. Blood—is that right ? "

Teddy Trimmer shook his head.

" No, Inspector."

Steady as a Rock frowned.

" Think carefully, man. The solution of the whole case may depend upon your answer. Are you quite certain that you were not brought a drink by a beautiful waitress with red hair and violet eyes ? "

" No," Trimmer replied. " But," he added suddenly, " that just describes the small boy who asked me for my autograph at the back of the pavilion."

" Did you give it to him ? "

" Yes."

Steady as a Rock paced for a moment silently, his brain racing. Then suddenly he shot the question, " Did you use your own pencil ? "

" No, the boy had one all ready."

Steady as a Rock smiled triumphantly.

" That's how it was done. The drug was

administered through the pencil. You licked
it ? "

" Yes. It didn't write very well."

" Ah. We're getting on. That woman with
red hair and violet eyes. First of all she mas-
queraded as a waitress and then as a small boy
autograph-hunting. It's clear to me that this
crime is the work of a clever and resourceful
gang."

Suddenly he was interrupted.

" By Gum, Chief! Look at this."

It was the finger-print expert who spoke.
He was very pale and he pointed, as he spoke,
to one of the photographs of old famous
cricketers surrounding the room. It was the
photograph of the oldest and most famous of
all the cricketers and across it were scrawled in
red letters the three ominous words,

" The Bad Men."

" Gosh ! " said Steady as a Rock Posse. " So
that's it, eh ? "

* * *

Play continued. The drugged men were
accorded an ovation when, as all the journalists wrote simultaneously, they " pluckily re-

sumed ". But despite their efforts, the English total amounted to only one hundred and thirty-one. And then in the evening light the Imperian opening pair, Thrust and Parry, put on fourteen runs without being separated.

The crowd dispersed at the end of that eventful day, full of foreboding for England's chances.

" There can be no two opinions about it.
The Bad Men must be caught."

*The Leader of the Opposition in a
week-end speech*

THE news that the drugging of members of the English team was the work of the Bad Men spread like wild-fire. It is not too much to say that the country throbbed with indignation. It was felt that a foul blow had been dealt at a cherished national institution.

At the time of the assassination of the President of Guamelia and also at the blowing up of the National Bank of Gloritana, the Bad Men had been regarded with a certain sympathy as brilliant and daring criminals facing tremendous odds. But this matter of interfering with a Test Match was felt to be in a different category altogether. All over England men and women discussed the outrage with horror and loathing. With a single voice the country demanded that the Bad Men must be brought to book.

Any suspicion that the Bad Men had been employed by the Imperians themselves was dispelled when Lethbridge issued a statement.

" I am profoundly shocked by today's events.

All Imperia will feel the same. Everyone is very fit. I still hope the best team will win."

The Sunday Press enjoyed the unique situation to the utmost. The *Sunday Weight* in its sober fashion advocated steadiness to its readers.

KEEP COOL
NO IMMEDIATE CAUSE FOR PANIC

The Bad Men, it said, were holding a pistol to the head of the nation. Hitherto their crimes, though regrettable, had been of a minor character and executed at a distance. Now they had struck at the very heart of our empire.

Although the general tone of the article was moderate and optimistic, it contained the striking warning, " We are only at the beginning of this match. What further incidents may be in store before the last ball is bowled, we cannot see. The future is veiled in obscurity. We must realize, however, that we are faced with a criminal organization of the utmost ruthlessness. They must be shown that we will not for a moment tolerate their gangster methods. There seems, however, no reason why, given general goodwill, we should not emerge from the long-drawn struggle and even find ourselves the victors."

Other papers dealt with the affair in their own characteristic fashion. It was represented as a dastardly attempt on the part of capitalist forces working through the Bad Men to wreck the simple pleasures of the working man. Conversely, it was shown to be a particularly sinister effort on the part of the communists to destroy the stately and solemn flow of English life.

Others again regarded it from a more personal and picturesque angle. The *Sunday Photograph* produced the arresting headlines :

DRUGGED AT THE WICKET
KEPT STRAIGHT BATS THOUGH SEMI-CONSCIOUS

It contained, too, a photograph of an infant Crigh holding a tiny bat, together with one of his mother, who, on being informed of her son's misfortune, had uttered the simple words,

"What, our Bill drugged ! What a shame ! "

Mrs. Hugh, also photographed and interviewed, had observed,

" I am very proud of our Fred."

The *Sunday Crime Sheet*, on the other hand, with its flair for riveting the attention of readers,

concentrated mainly upon the mysterious pur-
veyor of the drug.

**ENGLAND'S OPENING PAIR TAMPERED WITH
BY MODERN JEZEBEL.
RED-HAIRED TOOL OF BAD MEN
MASQUERADES AS WAITRESS.
THE AUTOGRAPH OF DOOM.**

" Who is the red-haired mystery-woman who
yesterday played havoc with the cream of
England's batting-strength ? What story of
degradation and shame lies behind the downfall of the poor abandoned creature who could
bring herself to commit this despicable act ?
Mothers of England, guard your daughters
well. Save them from such a life of shame."

It was learned, as the day wore on, that
extraordinary precautions were being taken.
A detachment of the Guards had been drafted
to the Oval ; day and night the pitch was surrounded. Sentries were posted at all the
entrances. Tanks, it was said, had been heard
rumbling through the streets of Kennington in
the early hours of Sunday morning. To each
one of the players a plain-clothes man had been
allotted with instructions not to leave him by
day or night until the match was concluded.

The great public reacted to the tense situation in normal fashion. Meetings were held in all possible places and heatedly addressed. A large crowd assembled outside the Oval to stare at the sentries ; a number of people assembled also in Downing Street. The latter had the satisfaction of seeing the Colonial Secretary, who had hurriedly returned from a shooting holiday in Scotland, arrive and enter Number 10. It was observed that the well-known features wore a smile and a wave of optimism passed over the watchers.

In the sanctity of the Cabinet Room Prime Minister and Colonial Secretary met and discussed the situation.

" Morning, P.M."

" Morning, C.S."

" Cigar ? "

" Thanks."

" Good of you to hurry back. How's the shooting ? "

" Fine. Why, yesterday morning, believe it or not——"

For a while the two statesmen conversed in this amicable manner. Presently the Colonial Secretary rose to go.

" Oh, by the way, P.M., about this Test Match business."

The Prime Minister waved his hand.

" That's your pigeon entirely, my dear chap. I have every confidence in your ability to handle it."

" Thanks very much. As far as I can see everybody is doing everything that can be done."

" I'm sure of it," replied the Prime Minister warmly. " I'll have a statement issued that His Majesty's Government are in full agreement."

" Fine. Splendid. It's a pleasure to work with a man like you. I'll make a point of mentioning in my speech at Basingstoke next month that unanimity among His Majesty's ministers has never been stronger."

" Do, my dear fellow. That always goes down well."

" It's always a blessing when these things happen when the House isn't sitting. None of those infernal questions. Well, well, I'll be off. I suppose, for the look of it, I'd better show up at the Oval tomorrow. Man on the spot and all that sort of thing. I think we ought to beat them, if we can get Lethbridge out. Our bowling is pretty good, you know. If only Truth can find a spot ! "

Something of a cloud settled upon the Prime Minister's hitherto serene brow.

" In my opinion," he said, " Prestwick should be playing."

The Colonial Secretary regarded him with amazement, not untinged with indignation.

" I entirely disagree," he replied sharply. " I dislike this modern mania for spin-bowling. Truth will supply all we want. If you ask me, a good fast medium bowler like Swerver of Gritshire is the man we want."

The Prime Minister smiled in the superior fashion which so greatly irritated Opposition leaders and out-of-work ex-cabinet ministers.

" Swerver ! An adequate stock bowler, no doubt, for county cricket purposes. Entirely lacking Prestwick's subtlety."

" Rubbish ! " snorted the Colonial Secretary rebelliously. " If I may say so, you don't know the first thing about bowling."

The Prime Minister smiled no longer. He was famous for his tolerance, but there are some insults which cannot be swallowed. Placing his feet upon the table and looking up abstractedly at the ceiling, he observed very coldly,

" The Right Hon. Member for Upper

Peebles is exceeding the limits of reasonable intercourse."

The Colonial Secretary was not to be out-done.

" I suggest," he replied, for he had had a legal training, " that the Prime Minister is not uninfluenced by the fact that he was born in Glebeshire."

The Prime Minister continued to stare at the ceiling.

" Shouts of withdraw," he murmured frigidly.

" I shall certainly not withdraw. I meant every word that I said. Why, dash it all, my dear Prime Minister——"

The Prime Minister's voice held the edge of a knife, as he interrupted,

" When people address me as ' My dear Prime Minister ' it is usually an indication that they are about to resign. Am I right in assuming that that is your intention ? "

" Certainly not," the Colonial Secretary replied hotly. " I never heard such nonsense. Why, I should have the entire Cabinet behind me over the question of Prestwick. You would be completely out-voted, and you know it. You would either have to knuckle under or else go to the country. Either would be fatal to you. And in my opinion quite rightly. If I may say so, a man who prefers Prestwick to Swerver is no longer capable of directing the affairs of a great empire."

The Prime Minister's reply was not in the best parliamentary tradition. Taking his feet off the table and sitting upright, he said curtly,

" Stuff and nonsense ! Swerver could not bowl out a preparatory school eleven."

" There is no need to get angry," replied the Colonial Secretary, feeling that he had scored a point. " I am talking the soundest sense and you know it. Moreover, I shall take the opportunity to make it perfectly clear at Basingstoke that, though outwardly unanimous, the Cabinet do not by any means always see eye to eye with one another on questions of the gravest importance."

" You can say what you like at Basingstoke," snapped the Prime Minister. " No-one takes your speeches seriously, anyway. How can they when you bring in that tag about the ' length and breadth of the land ' in every second sentence."

The Colonial Secretary, greatly hurt at this slighting reference to his oratorical powers, replied with deadly calm,

" There is no more to be said. I shall be present at the Oval tomorrow in conscientious discharge of my duties, and after that I shall return to Scotland to shoot."

" The sooner the better so far as I am concerned. But for heaven's sake don't be photographed again shooting in that ridiculous hat with the feather stuck in it. You look a perfect fool in that hat, in fact a menace to the whole stability of the party."

" I disagree. That hat is a human and personal touch. It endears me to the great masses of newspaper readers."

" On the contrary, it merely supplies cartoonists and music hall comedians with ready-made jokes. I wonder you have never seen that for yourself."

The Colonial Secretary was very pale and breathing hard, as he answered,

" Since we are speaking with the gloves off, Prime Minister, I will take this opportunity of saying here and now that I have never understood how your constituency or the country as a whole ever stood for that picture of you building a wall. It made you a laughing stock throughout the length and breadth—er, that is to say, all over the place. Even the veriest

138

nincompoop must have known that you didn't
in the least know what to do with the brick
you were clutching."

" It was a very good picture. Much more
full of human interest than your hat. At any
rate, I was doing something useful instead of
worrying inoffensive birds who haven't even
any political views. True the wall fell down
almost immediately, but I was setting an
example of industry and thrift. And I did
not wear a comic hat."

It is possible that this regrettable argument
would have endured for a considerable time,
but just then a knock came on the door. The
truth was that the Prime Minister had pressed
a secret bell three times which was the signal
for a secretary to enter with a despatch box
full of papers. The Prime Minister immediately assumed a weary air and began to study
them. The Colonial Secretary who knew all
about the trick, having seen it worked more
than once upon unwelcome visitors, withdrew
with a stiff bow.

When he appeared upon the door-step of
Number 10 the Colonial Secretary was seen to
be wearing a heavy frown. A wave of pessi-
mism immediately swept over the waiting

crowd. An enterprising journalist who contrived to get near enough overheard him mutter irritably,

" Dash it, the man is nothing but a pig-headed old fool."

Instantly the journalist wrote in his notebook the glad words,

CABINET SPLIT.

Upon the following morning his paper, which happened to be the *Daily Haywire*, was able to announce exclusively that, as a result of the events at the Oval, an important resignation was imminent, which would entail sweeping changes in the constitution of the Cabinet. That great newspaper thus secured another scoop.

The conference at Downing Street was not the only one which took place that day.

The Home Secretary impressed upon the Commissioner of Police that something must be done.

" All this," he said, " has aroused strong feeling in the country. Besides, I want to get away and take a cure. If the Bad Men aren't arrested, I shall have to stay in London until this wretched match is over. And if this chap,

Lethbridge, gets thoroughly set, it may last
until September."

" Surely," protested the Commissioner, " nothing really matters except that England should
win the match."

" Perhaps," replied the Home Secretary
bitterly, " you do not suffer from an acid
stomach. Besides, anyway, I was a rowing
man when I was up at Oxford. Please see
that something is done."

The Commissioner returned to the Yard and
informed the Big Six that something must be
done quickly.

The Big Six took counsel together. Since
yesterday's close of play the Yard had been
working at fever-heat. In an effort to find the
mysterious red-haired woman two hundred and
seventy-five indignant female crooks had been
pulled in, brought to the Yard and questioned
without mercy. All, however, had produced
unimpeachable alibis. At one time it had
been hoped to pin something on Champagne
Hetty, but her alibi had finally remained un-
shaken, or as they say, cast iron.

Shoot-first Mavis had also been under
considerable suspicion and Steady as a Rock
Posse had grilled her relentlessly. But she was

able to prove definitely that at the time of the Oval drugging she was acting as decoy for a smash and grab raid in an entirely different part of London. Steady as a Rock was forced reluctantly to let her go.

"I guess that lets you out, Mavis," he growled. "Heaven help you, if you're hiding up anything."

It must be confessed, then, that no material progress had been made with the case when Steady as a Rock faced his colleagues in conference. Before him lay the photographs of Hugh and Crigh in their prostrate condition, the only exhibit so far attained in this remarkable case.

"This is a difficult case, boys," he observed. "We've got to face it. We're up against the most dangerous gang in the world."

The others sucked their pipes and agreed gloomily.

"There's nothing to go on," said Who Dies if England Lives Narkley. "No body, no remains, no clues."

"The Bad Men," answered Steady as a Rock, "don't leave clues. Their leader is said to be a super-criminal, or what the late Sherlock Holmes called a Napoleon of Crime."

" Well, if it comes to that," countered And What is More You'll be a Man, my Son, Darby, " we are the Pride of the Yard so we ought to be equally matched. I never believed in this super-criminal business, anyway."

" If only there was a body ! " sighed Who Dies if England Lives Narkley. " Or even a few limbs in a parcel. I mean to say, that's something. As it is, I'm hanged if I can see where to start."

" As a start," suggested Dogged Does It Cordon, " we can watch the ports."

" They are still watching the ports in Guamelia," said I am the Captain of my soul Phillpots sadly, " and, I believe, in Gloritana."

" If you ask me," said What Can a Little Chap Do Tomkins, " it's a Secret Service job. That's the kind of thing the Bad Men go in for. We ought not to be mixed up in it all. Perhaps this red-haired girl is a celebrated female spy. Perhaps Hugh and Crigh were carrying important diplomatic papers."

" My dear fellow," replied Steady as a Rock testily, " men don't go in to bat in a Test Match carrying important diplomatic papers."

What Can a Little Chap Do Tomkins was about to answer warmly, but at this point the telephone rang. Dogged Does It Cordon answered it and reported to Steady as a Rock Posse.

" It's a message from the Oval."

" Ah ! Any news ? "

" The officer in charge says that amateur detectives of all sexes and nationalities keep arriving and demanding to have a look round. They are all quite certain they can catch the Bad Men. The officer wants to know if he can give his sentries orders to shoot."

A wistful look appeared on the face of Steady as a Rock Posse.

" It seems a pity," he said sorrowfully, " but I'm afraid the Old Man wouldn't stand for it."

" He says that a particularly infuriating young man called Mr. Chance has just arrived with a peculiarly loathsome line in comic back chat. The officer in charge seems to want to shoot him very much."

" I'm afraid he'll have to control himself," replied Steady as a Rock Posse. " Of course if one of his sentries happened to get a little excited . . . but I'm afraid we can't give him official permission. No, I'm very much afraid not. Now, boys, to get back to the case——"

The discussion proceeded without, however, advancing the case in the slightest degree.

The conference finally broke up without any line of action being agreed upon, except that the Big Six unanimously decided to drop all other cases in which they were engaged and be present at the Oval on the morrow.

*　　　*　　　*

Two conversations took place that day, which, had they been able to overhear them, would have enlightened the Big Six considerably.

One of these conversations took place in Golders Green between a middle-aged husband and wife of impeccable respectability.

The husband, who had just finished his breakfast, looked up from the *Sunday Crime Sheet* and remarked, " You know, my dear, I shouldn't be surprised if this mysterious red-haired woman that everyone is looking for, was our Alice."

It was the first time that the name of their errant daughter had been mentioned between them for some years.　The respectable mother winced.

" Could she have come to that, do you think ?
To drugging first-class cricketers ? "

" Who knows ? " replied her husband. " You
know what it is when girls start on the downward path. And certainly she had very red
hair."

" True," sighed his wife. " What a pity it
is that she was made Miss Bogpool-on-Sea for
1932 ! She was such a good girl before that
happened. Ah well, we might have guessed
what would come of it. Should we inform the
police, do you think ? "

" I don't think we need go as far as that, my
dear. In a way, I can't help feeling that we
are a little to blame for Alice's shame. Perhaps if we had gone to Bournemouth for our
fortnight that fatal summer. Besides, we do
not know for certain that it is Alice the police
are looking for . . ."

The other conversation took place in the
heart of Loamshire, whither the Bad Men had
repaired by separate routes at the conclusion
of Saturday's play. Here Sabbath calm prevailed, as the Professor and Ralph the Disappointment strolled a little before the old stone
house. All about them swept the deserted im-
mensity of the moors, the utter silence broken

only by the cries of the correct wild birds. From time to time upon the skyline appeared the form of a wild pony or an escaped convict from the great prison a few miles distant. But that was all. It was a scene of almost unbelievable desolation.

The smooth working of yesterday's plans had put the Professor in excellent spirits.

" Everything, my dear Ralph," he observed, pulling gently at one of his thin cigars, " proceeds according to plan. Our modest intervention in this absurd contest of crickets has already shaken the Empire to its foundations. I venture to think that when my plans are completed this affair will prove to be my masterpiece."

But Ralph the Disappointment failed to share his elation.

" I wish it were safely over," he said, and his voice trembled. " I cannot think that Providence will allow us to succeed in our dreadful purpose."

" Nonsense, good Ralph." The Professor's voice was almost gay. " My plans are far too subtle to admit of failure. Flash Alice is already safely out of the country and all goes well. Before the last shout of ' Chukka and

147

Tiffin !' has filled the Oval, the great English Sporting Public will have seen what the admirable L. E. G. Glance has described in his monumental work as a 'dramatic finish.' And now, excellent Ralph, with regard to Plan B, which I shall put into execution tomorrow . . ."

For a while he spoke in his dry, precise voice. The effect of what he said upon Ralph the Disappointment was remarkable. That unhappy man trembled violently as he listened and presently a hoarse cry broke from him.

" Professor, I cannot do this fearful thing. You ask too much of me. I am smirched, I know, with every kind of foulness ; I am, I readily admit, the filthiest of fellas, but that I cannot do."

As on a former occasion, the Professor did not stoop to argue. He merely said with dreadful softness,

" Look at me, Ralph."

The effect was the same as ever. Weakened will gave in to mighty will.

" Very well," Ralph groaned, his eyes dropping, " I will do as you say."

The Professor smiled.

" Listen then, Ralph. The Blood town

house is situated in the fashionable thorough-
fare known as Sleek Street . . ."

Back in the old stone house, meanwhile,
Sawn-off Carlo was writing a letter to his dear
old mother in her bum apoitment house in
New Yoick.

" DEAREST MOMMA,
" This England is sure a bum country. Do
the citizens hand you the dead pan or do they ?
It is also very old-fashioned. I haven't shot up
a guy in weeks and feel like I'm nothing but a
big sissy. Also Ralph the Disappointment says
this crime we are engaged in is not so good,
because it looks like the cops is getting all hit
up owing to them cricketing guys being doped,
because Ralph the Disappointment says it is
well known to one and all that you can dope
any guys in this country except cricketing guys,
them being regarded as the cat's lingerie. But
I guess them British Cops is dumb, anyway,
dearest momma, and the Big Shot knows his
onions. So what ?

" We gotta swell dame in this crime, dearest
momma. Her name is Flash Alice and has she
got plenty of this and that, or has she ? Oh,
boy. But the Big Shot says this jane has gotta
disappear, which is not so good, because had
that frail got swell curves or had she ? I'm
telling you.

" I hope that you are okay, dearest momma,

149

and that my little sister Guinevere is acting old-fashioned and not getting around with any smart guys since it is well known to one and all that us killers get sore when our blue-eyed little sisters start getting around with smart guys like Pietro the Wop, especially if they feel like they wanna fall for him in a big way, because we get thinking about our happy childhood days and then we get mad and start something and perhaps this smart guy gets ironed out to the grief of one and all.

"I see this English ball game yesterday, dearest momma. I guess a smart mortician could put on a snappier act.

"Goodbye, dearest momma, I'll be seeing you.

"Your tough but loving son,
"CARLO."

His artless epistle concluded, he shifted his gum from one side of his mouth to the other, and pulling a revolver from beneath his arm practised a few shots at imaginary cops. He was just a big simple-hearted fellow, and found an English Sunday in the heart of Loamshire not a little tedious.

When England first at Heaven's command
Taught other nations cricket
They used to spend three days at most
At or about the wicket.
But now by Heaven's command the game
Goes on and on and on.   The same
Batsmen appear each day to bat.
It may go on for weeks like that.
Nothing in short could well be drearier
Than timeless England *v.* Imperia.
(Oh, my God, keep me from going lunatic
There's no time limit in the Test.)

From *The Ancient Groundsman*

PLAN B

VERY early on Monday morning the sentries, stationed at the gates of the Oval, saw the first signs of the gathering of another enormous crowd. The sensational events of Saturday, together with the tension prevailing over the week-end, had whipped up public interest to fever heat. Would there be a repetition of Saturday's extraordinary scenes? Would these mysterious Bad Men strike again, and if so, how? Such topics swamped even the possibility of an enormous score on the part of Lethbridge.

Scotland Yard had ordained that everyone must be searched before entering the ground and this caused considerable delay—the last people, in fact, did not pass through the turn-stiles until it was almost time for the tea-interval—but the vast throng bore the discomfort with fortitude. It was realized that a crisis was in being and the multitude passed the long wait by singing patriotic songs. Early in the day the arrival of the players, each accompanied by a plain-clothes policeman, was loudly cheered. A small boy who, not understanding about the crisis, asked Hugh for his autograph was immediately arrested amid thunderous applause and cries of " He's one of the gang ", " Down with the Bad Men ! " and so on.

Within the ground an air of tension prevailed, even greater than that which had preceded the opening overs on Saturday. As the time for play drew near, the troops were withdrawn from the pitch. They marched smartly off the ground to the accompaniment of resounding cheers. It was noticed, however, that a large number of police had been drafted to the Oval ; they were stationed all round the playing area, greatly interfering with the view of the spectators. A further force was held in readiness behind the pavilion ready to be rushed to any point where their presence might be necessary. In the pavilion itself were to be seen the Colonial Secretary, somewhat embittered about the report of his impending resignation, as well as six massive stern-faced men smoking pipes and wearing bowler hats. It was to be observed that these men—none other than the Big Six—wore gaily striped ties, thus cleverly creating the illusion that they were famous cricketers.

Sir Timothy was very indignant about it and inquired coldly of Steady as a Rock Posse,

" Who are your friends ? "

" D.D.I. Cordon," answered Steady as a Rock promptly, "A. W. I. M. Y. B. A. M. M. S. Darby, W. D. I. E. L. Narkley and others. All famous ex-cricketers."

" I do not believe it," replied Sir Timothy. " Never in the course of my long and honourable career have I seen six famous cricketers sitting in a row wearing bowler hats. I believe these men to be detective friends of yours and I shall complain to the committee."

The conversation was not continued, for just then Norman Blood led his team out into the field, and a few minutes later Thrust and Parry, accompanied by two uniformed constables, marched to the wicket. A journalist wrote that they were surrounded by a battery of policemen, but subsequently crossed it out. It seemed to him to be nonsense, as indeed it was.

There is no need to describe in detail the events of that day. For, contrary to expectation, the game proceeded in normal fashion without sensational interruption and abler

writers have dealt with it. Both Mr. Beetling
Grim and Miss Felicia Portcullis wrote striking
accounts, and the voice of Mr. John Beltravers
penetrating all over England described the play
as it progressed. Let it suffice to say that England's bowlers, Truth and Frank Manleigh,
bowled with such subtlety and gusto that Imperia were all out by tea-time for 175 runs, of
which the indomitable Lethbridge had scored
89, remaining in the words of sixteen journalists, " undefeated at the close ".

Hugh and Crigh went again to the wickets,
and when Crigh was l.b.w. at 17, Norman
Blood himself went in. It was seen at once
that he was in an inspired mood. Carrying
on the good work of Truth and Frank Manleigh,
he attacked the bowling confidently, while
Hugh kept up his end with unshakable patience,
only falling to a catch at the wicket during the
last quarter of an hour of the day. At the close
of play England were fifty runs ahead with
eight wickets in hand. England had fought
back.

ALL QUIET ON THE OVAL FRONT screamed
the evening papers. **YARD FOILS TEST
WRECKERS.** And again, **BAD MEN AT BAY.**
But before the Big Six drove away in their

police car, they had seen the troops reoccupy the wicket, and the sentries posted at the gates. It was felt that Steady as a Rock Posse hit off the situation admirably when he remarked,

" In a case like this, the Yard leaves nothing to chance."

*   *   *

Dinner was over in the Blood town house. The port circulated ; the fragrance of good cigars filled the air.   Sir Timothy, reminiscent as always at this period of the evening, was relating to Norman, the Vicar and Monica, the story of how he had been run out by Josser Slingsby in 1894.

" And so there was I," he concluded his narrative, " when one short of the coveted three figures, as we used to call them in those days, on my way back to the pavilion, thanks to Josser Slingsby's stupidity. Josser never recovered.   It broke him up.   He never played again.   He spent his last years in a Home for Aged Cricketers under the delusion that he was a superannuated race-horse.   In a final flash of sanity he sent a message asking my forgiveness.   In order to ease his last moments

I forgave him, though, of course, I made it quite clear that there was never a possible run."

" Poor fellow," murmured Monica, her girlish eyes full of tears. " I can't help feeling sorry for him."

" He made his mistake," answered Sir Timothy sternly, " and he paid the price. Cricket is like that."

" Men must play and women must weep," sighed the Vicar. " I'm sure poor Josser would not have had things otherwise."

" He could not have continued to mix with cricketers on the old terms," said Sir Timothy. " Perhaps a man of stronger character would have shot himself at the time. Another glass of port, Vicar ? "

" Thank you, Sir Timothy, thank you. This, if I may say so, is a noble wine."

As the saintly old Vicar was in the act of pouring himself out another glass, the Blood butler entered the dining-room. He addressed himself to Norman.

" There is a masked man outside, Mr. Norman. He says that he comes from the Selection Committee who urgently need your presence."

" Very well, I'll come."

Norman excused himself, rose from the table and left the room.

Upon the pavement outside stood a burly figure, a soft hat pulled down over his eyes. Beneath the mask which he wore his jaws worked ceaselessly. A saloon car was drawn up by the kerb ; a second masked man sat at the wheel. Norman had no suspicion that anything was amiss. He knew well the Selection Committee's love of secrecy. Nothing was more likely than that they should send a closed car and two masked men to fetch him. Accordingly he addressed the stranger with his usual frankness.

" You come from the Selection Committee ? "

" Sure, brother. Step inside, big boy."

Still unsuspicious Norman obeyed. Instantly the car slid forward down Sleek Street. It was then that Norman felt something hard poking into his ribs ; and a voice in his ear said,

" You're in a tough spot, buddy. If you don't wanna hand in your dinner-pail, better act old-fashioned and don't try to pull a fast one. Likewise keep your puss shut or I'll sure give you the heat."

The unwelcome truth burst upon Norman in an instant.   He had been hoaxed.

*   *   *

There had been an unobserved witness of this scene, a male figure, who at the first appearance of the car had slunk out of sight. Nevertheless he had overheard the conversation between the bogus messenger from the Selection Committee and Norman Blood. Now, as the car moved forward, the watcher, obviously an athlete to his finger-tips, sprang for the back of it, clambered on to the luggage-grid and hung on grimly.

This unseen watcher was none other than Joe Prestwick, who, strictly speaking, should not have been in this part of London at all.   It was his great love which had brought him to Sleek Street.   Since he learned that he was to be twelfth man at the Oval Joe had not seen Monica.   She had written him a girlish note expressing her grief, to which he had replied in manly style.

" We must accept the decision of the Selection Committee, my darling, and remember that the most important thing of all is to beat

Imperia. I keep biting my lips a good deal and clenching and unclenching my fists in unrestrained fashion, but we must remember that perhaps the wicket would not have suited me. Goodbye, dearest Monica. I shall always keep the belt and remember your extraordinary radiance. Your broken-hearted unselected Joe."

So he had taken his leave of her. All the same he could not forbear to take his stand outside the Blood house at night and gaze up at the windows behind which his divinity lived and moved. He had been able to slip away from the other players at the hotel without difficulty, since no-one bothered to guard the twelfth man.

He had been standing thus on the pavement of Sleek Street, gaping at the lighted windows, when the mysterious car drove up. Lover's thoughts were instantly driven from his mind by the conversation he overheard. Unlike Norman Blood, he read books and frequently visited the pictures, and the truth flashed across his mind. Something was wrong. This big man in the mask did not speak like a messenger from the Selection Committee ; on the contrary, he spoke like all the crooks of whom Joe had ever heard. He saw it all. The villains who had drugged Hugh and Crigh were trying to do away with England's captain. Instinctively, just in time, he sprang for the back of the car.

For a moment, as the car sped up Sleek Street, an unworthy thought passed through his mind. If Norman Blood were not at the Oval tomorrow, when it was England's turn to field, the twelfth man would be called upon. He would play for England and be able to claim Monica.

Only for a moment, however, did this shameful thought occupy his mind. He dismissed it instantly. At all costs he must rescue Norman Blood. At all costs Norman Blood must be at the Oval tomorrow. Goodbye, Monica.

He bit his lips fiercely, but could not clench and unclench his fists, because of the necessity of hanging on to the luggage-grid.

The car sped on through the night.

*　　*　　*

On and on through the night sped the car. London presently was left behind ; they were

out upon the Great South East Road, heading
for what strange secret destination ?

So Norman Blood wondered, as he sat silent,
a prey to the bitterest thoughts.   If he were not
at the Oval tomorrow to finish his innings and
captain the side !   A thrill of despair passed
through him at the thought.   He upbraided
himself savagely.   What a fool to allow himself
to be hoaxed !   He had let down the team.
He was unworthy to be captain of England.
And yet, on reflection, it was difficult to see
how he could have acted otherwise.   The
scheme to abduct him had been so devilishly
subtle.   What more natural than that these
mysterious masked messengers had come from
the Selection Committee ?   Then he thought
again of the morrow.   What would his brave
boys think of him, if he were not there to lead
them when play began ?   What would the
great world of cricket lovers think if England's
captain must be marked in the score-book
" retired abducted " ?   A groan escaped him
at the shocking thought.

" Say, brother," remarked his companion,
who still held the revolver against his ribs,
" you sure don't sound so good.   Shall I give
you the story how I rub out Al Camponoli ? "

" Certainly not," replied Norman coldly.

" It's nice woik the way I plug that sap. I guess I get Al's stomach like it was an iron-monger's store."

" I do not wish," said Norman with angry disdain, " to have any conversation with a villain like you."

" Okay, big boy." His companion sighed and chewed for a moment in silence, before he added, " You folk sure hand a guy the dead pan."

Norman made no reply, partly because he did not understand this method of conversation, which was so different from that of his fellow-cricketers, partly because he was plunged again in bitter thoughts.

On and on, hour after hour, the car purred on its way. The surroundings had long since become quite unfamiliar to Norman. They tore through busy well-lit towns, through shuttered villages, along deserted country roads, the silent, masked driver picking his way with unerring precision. And gradually, it seemed to Norman, the aspect of the country through which they passed grew wilder and wilder. Towns, even villages, grew more scarce.

On and on, hour after hour—whither ? And

every hour, Norman reckoned desperately, took them forty or fifty miles farther from the Oval. Those fatal words " retired abducted " seemed to dance before his eyes in letters of flame.

It must have been well after midnight, when the car drew up before a small stone house in the loneliest part of a vast moor. Obeying a command from his captor, who still kept the gun close into his ribs, Norman descended from the car and walked towards the house. A single glance about him told him that there was small hope of finding help in this abandoned spot.

They passed through the door of the house and came into a small ground-floor room, where sat a strange, hooded figure. Though Norman could see nothing of his face he was strangely aware of a dominating, magnetic personality.

" Good evening, Mr. Blood," said a thin precise voice from below the hood. " You and I are going to have a little talk."

Norman folded his arms with quiet dignity.

" I do not think we have anything to talk about."

" Certainly," replied the precise voice, " we are going to talk about this match of crickets."

165

Norman shuddered, but did not answer. The voice from below the hood went on, sinking now into a dreadful threatening softness,

" If you value your life and liberty, Mr. Blood, I think you will be wise to give me your promise, as an Englishman and a cricketer, that Imperia shall win the match."

★　　　★　　　★

Outside the window crouched Joe Prestwick. He had not dared to leave his place of concealment until the masked driver had also disappeared into the house. He had trembled for a moment lest he should be discovered, but the driver did not come round to the back of the car. On the contrary, somewhat to Joe's surprise, he stood for a moment as though in deep and painful thought and then with an almost tragic sigh of,

" Heavens, what a filthy fella I am ! " followed the others inside.

Joe descended and looked about him. Beneath the stars he could see nothing but a vast expanse of empty moor. He guessed from the look of the scenery that he was somewhere in the heart of Loamshire.

Cautiously he crept towards the house and crouching beside the window peered in. The spectacle which met his eyes was one to daunt any patriotic cricketer. In a small room stood Norman Blood, face to face with a small, hooded figure whose veiled aspect somehow suggested extraordinary menace, while the burly, masked man whom Joe had seen on the pavement of Sleek Street kept him covered with a revolver. The masked driver who had sighed so deeply was not there.

" I felt sure," Joe reflected, " that those men were not genuine members of the Selection Committee. How glad I am that I jumped up behind the car ! "

But for the moment he was helpless. He could do nothing but crouch there, awaiting a chance to help his captain.

Sense, of late
Is out of date.

It is enough
To be tough.

Literary Ballad

EXTRACT FROM THE DIARY OF
SAWN-OFF CARLO

So we get this cricketing palooka to the Boss's hide-out in this place called the heart of Loamshire. He keeps his kisser closed in the auto like I say, but this is a great grief to me since, as I tell my dear old Momma, I ain't given a guy the heat in weeks and maybe I'll be losing the way of it. When I was around with Alfredo the Bum I used to rub out two or three suckers a week, and a guy sure gets the habit and feels kinda sissy when he's not qualifying for the Hot Seat. They fried Alfredo the Bum for the Doughberg Killing to the grief of one and all. Alfredo the Bum was a great guy and knew his onions.

So the auto stops and I say to this cricketing palooka,

"Step out, brother, pronto, and don't start anything because your happy young life don't mean a thing to me."

So we ease along into the hide-out, and there we find the Big Shot sitting all hooded up so this Blood guy won't see his face, and looking like he was the Boss of the Ku Klux Klan.

" Good evening, Mr. Blood," says the Big Shot.

Maybe this Blood guy knows he's in a tough spot, but he sure puts on a swell act.   He folds his arms and looks at the Big Shot old-fashioned. He is wearing a tuxedo and looks like a guy outside a dime novel.   Maybe he thinks presently he'll pull a fast one, but I got him covered.

" Now," says the Big Boss, " I wanna talk to you, Mr. Blood."

But this Blood guy calls the Big Boss an old-fashioned name, because it is plain to one and all that he is plenty hit up about our not being certain punks known as the Selection Committee.

" See here, Boss," I say, " let me beat up this guy, pronto."

But the Big Boss says, " Restrain your boyish enthusiasm, Carlo.   Me and Mr. Blood are going to have a little talk."   So he says to this Blood guy that if he promises to rig the ballgame, so the Imperians win, he'll let him go, and everything will be okay and hunky-dory. That gets the guy plenty sore.

" How dare you suggest such a thing ! " he says. " I would rather die."

" Maybe you'll have to, my young friend," says the Big Boss very nasty.

" Let me give him the woiks, Boss," I say. " I gotta kinda wistful feeling I'd like to croak that guy."

But the Boss says no we'll put him in the cellar because he'll have time to think and maybe before long he'll get the idea that he'd like to change his mind, and anyway he won't be around tomorrow when the ball-game starts. And it is plain to one and all that England will be in a tough spot with their captain not around, in fact it will not be so good.

" Do your worst," says this Blood guy, very highbrow. " I will never let down my side."

" Okay," says the Big Boss. " Sew him up."

So Ralph the Disappointment comes in and we tie the guy up good and tight and put a gag in his kisser, and carry him down to the cellar. And the Boss says to me I am to stay and guard him all night.

So there I am guarding this cricketing guy and everything is hunky-dory. But it is not so snappy guarding a guy who is all sewed up and can't talk any. So presently I get to thinking

173

about my aged mother, since it is well-known to one and all that us killers are sentimental guys and often get thinking about our aged mothers, especially if these aged mothers are grey-haired dames with sweet expressions, and my aged mother has got an expression so sweet a guy could tell without difficulty that she was a killer's aged mother.

Well, there I am thinking plenty about my aged mother and the tears come into my eyes because I am such a sentimental guy, and then I get thinking about my pure young sister and wondering whether I shall have to shoot up any swell guys when I get home. Especially if any guy has been giving my pure young sister jewellery, since it is well known to one and all that when a guy gets around giving jewellery to pure young dolls, it is not so good, and there is nothing for the pure young doll's loving brother to do but give this guy the heat in a big way. To wit bang bang.

Well, then I get thinking about my childhood days and how I croak my baby brother Benjamino with a penknife, and then I get very sentimental indeed because there is nothing that makes a guy so sentimental as thinking about his childhood's days.

So there I sit with the tears running down my face, and presently I think I'd like a drink, because nothing makes a guy so thirsty as feeling sentimental about his childhood's days. So I leave this cricketing sap all sewed up on the floor, and go upstairs. The Big Shot has gone to bed and everything is okay and hunky-dory. I mix myself a highball, or maybe two or three, and think some more about my innocent childhood, and presently I remember the cricketing palooka all sewed up downstairs. So I ease back to the cellar. And there is the guy all sewed up okay and everything is hunky-dory. So then I sit down and guard him some more.

It is after daylight when presently the Big Shot eases in and says is everything okay. Okay, Boss, I says. Then the Boss goes and looks at this cricketing guy and presently he uses an old-fashioned word.

" What's biting you, Boss ? " I says.

" You poor mutt," he says very nasty. " This is the wrong guy. Where's Norman Blood ? "

Well, it seems to me that one cricketing guy is much like another, but the Boss is sure mad. He pulls off the guy's gag and says,

" Who in heck are you ? "

So it seems that this guy is a sap called Prestwick, and it seems like he unsewed this Blood palooka while I was upstairs thinking about my innocent childhood and my pure young sister and this and that. And the Boss is sore because this Blood guy has made a getaway and will be able to muscle in on this ball-game again.

" You poor mutton-headed fool," he says to me, together with some other nasty cracks of a discouraging nature. " You have ruined my carefully thought-out plans."

" See here, Boss," I says, " if a guy calls me names like that his loving relations are around next day ordering flowers. If you had let me croak that Norman Blood guy, instead of fooling around with this highbrow super-criminal stuff everything woulda been okay and hunky-dory."

" You're telling me," he says still nasty.

" Yeah," I answered, " I'm telling you."

The Big Shot looks at me very old-fashioned.

" It's my own fault," he says. " I ought never to have employed a poor mutt like you in a high-class international crime."

Well, that gets me sore and I feel like I'm

ready to give the Boss the well-known stream of lead, like I give Al Camponoli and other disobliging characters, but the Big Shot goes on talking,

" We gotta scram outer here good and quick. This Blood guy will set the dicks on this hideout. I'll give this punk a shot of something to keep his puss shut. Then we'll beat it."

So he tells Ralph the Disappointment to get the auto ready and we're going to beat it. But it seems this Blood palooka has gotten into our auto and made his getaway, so it looks like we're in a tough spot, because it is plain to one and all that the G-men will be here pronto and that is not so good. So the Boss looks very mysterious and says, " We must use It now, instead of waiting for Plan C." And then he says some more about us being caught like rats in a trap, if we don't use It pronto. And once again he calls me an old-fashioned name because he says I mess up Plan B. And Ralph the Disappointment also hands me one or two nasty cracks of a similar nature. In fact it seems I am loathed and despised by one and all.

Now all this is very painful to me, because if I hadn't got around thinking of my aged

177

mother and this and that, this Blood palooka would never have made his getaway in our auto, and everything woulda been okay and hunky-dory. But I guess a guy has gotta feel sentimental sometimes, especially a guy like me who as is well-known to one and all has gotta great big hearta gold. And I guess if some of us quick-shooting guys hadn't got great big heartsa gold and didn't get all hit up when they thought about their aged mothers, the movies and the tough writers might as well go out of business.

So what ?

If, when making up a book,
You invent a super-crook
Always let him get away
You'll need that guy again some day.

From *Technique for the Toddlers* or
Earn Big Money During Infancy

ESCAPE

It is impossible to do justice to the mortification
and despair felt by Norman Blood as he lay
bound and gagged in the cellar beneath the
eyes of Sawn-off Carlo. Never, perhaps, since
the day when he scored a duck in his first
Gentlemen *v.* Players Match had life seemed
so black. His gloomiest predictions had come
true. Unless a miracle occurred, it would be
impossible for him to resume his innings at the
Oval at the appointed hour. His fevered
imagination pictured the ringing of bells, the
clearance of the ground, the solemn entry of
the umpires, followed by the Imperian fieldsmen. And then—the incredible news would
go about the Oval that England's Captain was
not there. Rage caused him to tremble all
over again, as he thought of the foul proposal
put forward by the mysterious hooded man,
that he should allow Imperia to win the Test
Match. The man, Norman concluded, must
be a madman, one of those madmen, no doubt,
whose brain worked with devilish perverted

cunning. No-one, surely, but a lunatic would put forward such a plan.

Slowly the dark hours went by and he was helpless. He could not even appeal to the sporting instincts of this big man who sat guarding him, for the gag in his mouth precluded any form of speech.

"Never despair," he repeated to himself, "a game is not won until it is lost," together with other tags of an optimistic nature which he had found helpful in many a tight corner on the cricket field. But now they brought him little comfort. There was no hope anywhere. So plunged was he in bitter gloom that he hardly noticed that presently his burly guard got up and left the room. Indeed, how could this help him, since he could not move hand or foot?

"I am as surely out of this match," he groaned aloud, "as if Bumper had clean bowled me."

He could scarcely believe his ears when he heard a familiar voice whisper,

"All right, Skipper. It's me. Prestwick (J.)."

For a moment he suspected another trick. These blackguards who had impersonated the

Selection Committee were equally capable of impersonating a rising young professional. But a glance showed him that it was indeed Joe. In a few moments Norman's bonds were torn off and he was free.

" What on earth are you doing here ? " he gasped.

Joe blushed.

" I happened to be on the back of the car, Skipper. I've been hanging about waiting for a chance to get to you. Just now I noticed that the man who has been guarding you was upstairs having a drink. I thought I'd take a chance. Luckily the cellar door was unlocked. You must get away now, Skipper. To the Oval."

" Have you any idea where we are ? "

" I think we are in the heart of Loamshire. One of the minor counties," he added, as Norman Blood looked puzzled.

" Ah yes, I remember. A curious egg-shaped place. I think they have a wicket-keeper named Huggins. F. Huggins."

" Yes, yes. But you must get away, Skipper. The car is still outside. Take it and drive like mad for London and the Oval. I'll stay here and take your place."

" Why not," Norman asked, " come with me ? "

But Joe argued eagerly,

" No.   I've thought it all out.   If they come and find no one here they will see that the game is up, but if they see a lifeless form of some sort the villains may not suspect any-thing.   They will remain here and that may give the police a chance to catch them.   When you get to the nearest town, go to the police station and telephone to Detective-Inspector Posse at the Yard.   We want to exterminate these enemies of England."

Norman Blood without further argument held out his hand.

" You are a noble fellow, Prestwick.   I will tie you up."

" Quickly, Skipper, before anyone comes back."

In a very short while Joe lay gagged and bound.   Norman Blood prepared to take his leave.

" Goodbye, Prestwick," he said in farewell, " I shall never forget this.   And by the way, it doesn't matter about that chance you failed to accept in the Gritshire match.   At least, not very much."

Joe could not speak, because he was gagged, but his eyes expressed his gratitude. Norman Blood stole away.

He passed through the door and crept up a short flight of steps into a passage. All was in darkness. He paused to listen, determined that if any of the villains, who had so basely posed as the Selection Committee, discovered him he would sell his life dearly. There was no sound, however. He crept on towards the front door. In another moment he was in the open air.

The big car still stood at the front door. He jumped in, started up, and within a few moments was driving across the moor in the growing daylight.

*   *   *

Steady as a Rock Posse was asleep. It is difficult to imagine that massive and majestic man lacking the symbols of his office, which struck terror into the hearts of the criminal classes, his bowler hat, his pipe, his ever-ready notebook. But even that tireless machine of a man required rest, and it is satisfactory to note that, even while unconscious, his face wore

185

its accustomed stern, set expression. Only occasionally a little smile of satisfaction, which upon the face of one of less solid and un- relenting character, might have been called a smirk, disturbed the set expression of his features. For like lesser men, Steady as a Rock dreamed.

Rosily he dreamed that he had " pulled in " the Bad Men. Exactly by what dazzling stroke of police work he had achieved this triumph was misty in his dream, but the scene itself was very clear. The super-criminal, for whom the police of half Europe had hunted in vain, cowered before him while he cross-examined him in his characteristic manner, so famous at the Yard.

" So you admit that you had Hugh and Crigh drugged, eh ? Come on, spill it ! "

The super-criminal cracked beneath the relentless fire of questions and confessed.

" I have defied," he whimpered in broken accents, " the police of half the world. But this man, Posse, is too hot for me."

" Put the darbies on him, boys," said Steady as a Rock. " The Test Match case is over."

The news of his triumph was received with acclamation. Constables all over the metro-

politan area shouted aloud, " Three cheers
for Posse!" No less a personage than the
Commissioner observed with emotion in his
voice,

" It would be hypocrisy upon my part to
remain at the head of an institution which
contains a man of Posse's ability. I resign
at once and hand over my exalted office to
him."

His colleagues of the Big Six crowded about
him, hands extended in congratulation, and
he answered with manly modesty,

" It is the Yard that matters, boys, not
me . . ."

Steady as a Rock's dream had reached this
interesting and satisfactory climax, when he
was rudely torn from it by the shrill note of the
telephone. Instantly his trained senses were
on the alert. A call was being put through to
him from the Yard. And soon he was wondering if he were not still dreaming, as he listened
to the story of Norman Blood's adventures and
learned that even now Prestwick, England's
twelfth man, lay bound and gagged in the
heart of Loamshire.

" Loamshire ? " echoed Steady as a Rock in
surprise.

" A minor county," Norman's voice explained, " shaped like an egg. They have a wicket-keeper named F. Huggins."

Steady as a Rock flashed the question,

" Do you suspect that this egg-shaped Huggins is one of the Bad Men ? "

" Good heavens, no. He is the Loamshire wicket-keeper. Chap with a little moustache. Not at all a bad bat, either, when he gets going. But in any case it's not Huggins who is the shape of an egg, it's the county."

" What has this Huggins to do with the crime ? "

" Nothing whatever. I'm just trying to explain to you about Loamshire. It's a beastly place, anyway. I don't wonder it never got among the first-class counties."

" Now, just let me have the chief facts, Mr. Blood."

A few quick rasped out questions and Steady as a Rock had made his plans. To the Local Inspector he gave orders that all available men must be rushed at once to the spot and the stone house surrounded.

Then, still from his bedside, he called up the Chief Constable of Loamshire. The Chief Constable's senses were not at first so clear as

Steady as a Rock's, but presently he appeared to grasp the situation.

" The Bad Men ?   I say, they're the blighters who are foolin' about with the Test Match."

" That's it, sir.   If we act swiftly we've got 'em.   I want every available man in Loamshire out on the moors at once.   Everyone is to be arrested at sight.   There must be no loopholes anywhere.   I'm coming down myself at once."

Within a few minutes Steady as a Rock, having dressed himself and explained to a bewildered Mrs. Posse that he was about to make a dramatic dash for Loamshire to achieve the greatest triumph of his career, was on his way to the Yard.   Quarter of an hour later, with two carefully picked men behind him in the police car, he had begun his dramatic dash for Loamshire.

Almost exactly half-way he passed Norman Blood, who was making a dramatic dash for the Oval.

They passed each other with stern, set faces, eyes relentlessly fixed upon the road ahead.

On arrival at Loamshire, Steady as a Rock found the vast expanse of moor almost entirely covered with policemen.   No-one, however,

had been seen or arrested. He continued his
dash towards the old stone house.

Here he found the local Inspector, with a
number of his own men, conscientiously surrounding the building.

" This is the place, sir," said the Inspector.
" There's no sign of anyone, but maybe they're
still inside. No-one has passed in or out."

" Stand back," exclaimed Steady as a Rock,
unable to keep a thrill of excitement out of his
voice. " I'm going in."

Followed by three or four stout men he entered the house. Through every room he passed
courageously, methodically. It was quite
deserted except for the luckless Joe, who was
still bound and under the influence of the drug.

" The birds have flown," snapped Steady as
a Rock, aptly if a little tritely.

No clue of any kind was to be found except
several lumps of discarded chewing-gum which
Steady as a Rock put carefully away in small
envelopes, a few bullet-holes in the walls of the
sitting-room and an envelope which lay in a
prominent position upon the table. Steady as
a Rock picked it up and tore it open.

The envelope contained a single sheet of
paper on which was scrawled a short message.

"We shall meet again at the Oval: The Bad Men."

*　　　*　　　*

The bell was ringing for the ground to be cleared when Norman Blood steered the purloined car through the gates of the Oval. Springing out he made a dash for the pavilion, brushing aside anxious questions as he went. Thank Heaven he had just time to plunge into flannels and pads and take his place at the wicket!

On entering the pavilion he encountered his father.

"Well, well, my boy," said Sir Timothy. "That was certainly a pretty lengthy meeting of the Selection Committee."

"Father," Norman replied, "I cannot tell you all now. But that masked messenger who called at our house last night was an impostor. I was kidnapped and imprisoned in the heart of Loamshire."

"Good heavens!" exclaimed Sir Timothy. "The heart of Loamshire! Well, really this match is the most extraordinary that I ever remember."

" The concluding stages were packed with thrills."

From thirty-seven separate accounts
of the match

PLAN C

THE welcoming cries of " Good old Norman ! " were music in the ears of Norman Blood as, with little Teddy Trimmer at his side, he walked to the wicket. He thought how but for Joe Prestwick's gallant sacrifice he would have been at this all-important moment lying helpless in the cellar on the Loamshire moors. Despite his nocturnal adventures he felt in good fettle. He was grimly determined to win the match for England and thus foil his enemies of last night. Something of his determination seemed to communicate itself to the crowd for they cheered him all the way to the wicket.

But that morning's cricket was sadly disappointing. England's wickets tumbled. Teddy Trimmer was almost immediately adjudged l.b.w., young Gayheart had his wickets spreadeagled before he had scored. The others followed in a disconsolate procession. Only Norman Blood stood firm. Disdaining his flashing strokes, he concentrated on rock-like defence. " Captain's innings " wrote thirty-five journalists.

Shortly after lunch the last wicket fell. Imperia had only to get one hundred and twenty-two to win. England's supporters, surrounding the pitch during the interval, were disconsolate. It seemed an easy task.

But it was soon seen that the match was by no means over. In the very first over of the Imperian innings there was a confident shout of appeal and Thrust was seen returning to the pavilion, caught at the wicket. 0–1–0. Lethbridge came in, looking stern.

" England," said Mr. Beltravers, " are definitely on the offensive. It is still anyone's game . . . "

Slowly runs came, the batsmen taking no chances. Lethbridge, like Norman Blood before him, was content to defend and score by singles. But the score inexorably mounted. 25–1–0.

" Back-to-the-wall stuff," said Mr. Beltravers to listening England. " Every ball full of drama . . . "

And then listening England heard a mighty roar as Parry fell, clean bowled by Manleigh. " He's OUT," cried Mr. Beltravers. " Parry is out. Bowled by a real beauty. Well, well, this is exciting stuff . . . "

Slowly, grimly the struggle went on, the English fieldsmen crouching almost at the end of the bat, the English bowlers, Truth and Frank Manleigh, exerting their greatest efforts. More wickets fell, but indomitable Lethbridge remained.

Tea Score. Imperia, 77 for 6. Lethbridge, not out 44. In English hearts new hope was growing.

At five o'clock Lethbridge reached his fifty, at five-ten the seventh wicket fell, ninety-two runs on the board. At five-twenty the hundred went up. At a quarter to six Gayheart made a remarkable catch, falling prostrate to hold the ball, and the eighth wicket fell with the total one hundred and fifteen. Two wickets to fall, seven runs to make.

The Imperian wicket-keeper entered, and off his first ball inadvertently scored a boundary. But three runs required to win. A single and the Imperians were one run behind. And then, with the last ball of the over, Manleigh sent the wicket-keeper's off-stump cartwheeling.

The last man, Bumper, Imperia's burly fast

bowler, came in amid an extraordinary silence. No batsman, Bumper, as all the world knew, but could he keep up his end, while Lethbridge scored the required runs ? In any case, Lethbridge had the bowling.

The tension became appalling. In the Press-box Miss Felicia Portcullis, through sheer nervousness, kept muttering aloud, " Lean bronzed men, lean bronzed men," to the great annoyance of Mr. Beetling Grim, who found himself incorporating this unsuitable phrase in his own account of these concluding moments. Mr. John Beltravers was practically speechless with excitement. In the pavilion Sir Timothy gnawed his moustache ; even the doyen of cricket could not in all his vast experience recall so close a finish. Monica had absent-mindedly snatched off the hat of the man next to her and was lightly swinging it, while her saintly old father repeated aloud large sections of the marriage service. In a stand near the Vauxhall end a Bishop was sick.

Bumper reached the wicket. One run to make to equal England's score, one wicket to fall and Lethbridge facing the bowling. The fieldsmen went to their stations. Truth stood nervously tossing the ball from hand to hand.

*   *   *

And then it was that the amazing thing happened.

In the general tension which prevailed the drone of the approaching airplane was hardly noticed. Even when the machine circled low above the Oval, little attention was paid to it, for behind it a deceptive streamer fluttered out, bearing the slogan, " Keep that Schoolgirl Fragrance."

Here and there old-fashioned people muttered about the intrusion of modern advertising methods, but that was all. No-one anticipated what was about to happen. Once, twice the airplane circled low above the heads of the players and then just as the fielders were in place for Truth's historic over, it suddenly dived. A great gasp went up from thousands of throats, as for the first time during an important match at the Oval there was heard the deadly rattle of a machine-gun.

The astonishing events of the next few minutes may be best described in the words of Mr.

John Beltravers, as they were heard all over the country, in mansion and cottage, on portable sets, by spellbound parties at the seaside and by horror-stricken chauffeurs sitting tensely in expensive cars.

"By Jove," said Mr. Beltravers, "this is extraordinary. I never remember anything like this on a cricket ground before. The plane is diving down towards the pitch. There are three men in her. They must be the Bad Men. They've got masks on. But I can see from here that one of them has a tremendously magnetic personality. One of them seems to be chewing something. Yes, through my glasses I can see his jaws working. He's the chap at the gun. He's shooting now. I expect you can hear. One, two, three, four. All the players are lying full length on the ground. Blood at cover, Hugh at mid-off, Crigh in the gully. No, I'm sorry, Gayheart in the gully ; it's a little hard to tell when they're all lying flat. Crigh seems to be trembling a little, but Hugh looks just as kingly as ever. . . . Here's the plane diving again. I can see the man leaning out, still chewing. He shoots. A long burst. By George, he's got Trimmer. He's DEAD. No, he's not. He's rolling over. My word, that must have been a near thing. Fortunately this fellow's shooting is not very accurate. Hostile, but not accurate. He hasn't found a length yet. Well, really, this is all tremendously exciting. There's an old man over there standing up and waving a panama hat. I can see several women fainting. Up in the Pressbox Miss Felicia Portcullis, the well-known novelist, has just uttered a tremendous scream . . . Hullo, here are the Guards doubling out. They've got their rifles. They're going to shoot. Splendid fellows, these Guards, equipment beautifully clean, buttons winking in the sun. The airplane gives them a burst, but they don't mind. They're opening fire. And here come a couple of tanks waddling along from the pavilion end. Well, this must be absolutely a record . . . "

Spellbound the crowd watched that strange struggle. They saw the detachment of Guards double out of the pavilion, shake out into line and open rapid fire upon the marauding airplane.

A cheer went up from the more unthinking section of the crowd, as the tanks came into play, their guns blazing, but in the pavilion the gravest fears were expressed. Q. E. D. Marjoribanks said gloomily,

" Something of this kind was bound to happen sooner or later when they raised that foolish cry about brighter cricket."

And R. S. V. P. Hatstock agreed,

" It's bad enough when fellows suggest that the ball should be smaller and the wickets larger, but — really — flying-machines and machine-guns and tanks !   It's not cricket."

As for Sir Timothy, he was beside himself with indignation. Springing up, his fine old face purple with anger, he rushed down the pavilion steps, shouting,

" Take that ridiculous aeroplane away. This is a cricket match not a revolution. We're not in foreign parts now."

Several people rushed to hold him back, explaining that he was exposing himself to great danger.

" I would rather," declared the Grand Old Man, " see myself dead at my own feet than a cricket match interfered with in this abominable foreign fashion. Tell them to take that aeroplane away."

Hotter and hotter grew the fire of the Guards and the tanks. And presently a great shout went up as it was seen that the airplane was making off. Away it roared over the heads of the spectators at the Vauxhall end, its streamer, with the words, " Keep that Schoolgirl Fragrance ", floating out behind it. A final volley of rifle-fire followed it.

" The enemy plane is making off at full speed," announced Mr. Beltravers. " The Guards are coming back into the pavilion. The players will be getting up in a minute, I expect. Ah, yes, the umpires are just cautiously raising their heads . . ."

All over England a sigh of relief went up. The dastardly attack had been beaten off.

*   *   *

When at length, following a little good-natured barracking from the spectators—for an English crowd never loses its sense of humour —the players rose cautiously to their feet, it was observed that all were unscathed save Trimmer who had been slightly hit in the leg. Amid sympathetic cheers and cries of " Got a blighty one, Teddy ? " he was carried from the ground.

Monica all through this strange battle had been excitedly swinging her neighbour's hat. Although bullets were flying about the Oval in

this alarming manner, she was determined
that she would be splendid and keep her
head and not start a panic. For she knew
that when women and children kept cool,
even cowardly men were shamed into a show
of courage.

" Keep cool," she said firmly to her neighbour. " Don't panic. We shall pull through."

" I don't know what on earth you are talking
about," answered the man irritably.

" Oh," replied Monica earnestly, " I'm just
being splendid."

" I can't say that I see it," he said rudely.
" And I wish you'd give me back my hat."

" What is going on ? " inquired the saintly
old Vicar, perceiving that something of an
argument had arisen.

" This young lady," the man said, " insists
on being splendid with my hat. It's a most
irritating habit."

" The younger generation," the Vicar replied
peaceably, " are often impulsive. But their
hearts are in the right place."

" It would be more to the point," the man
said, " if my hat was in its right place, which
in my opinion is on my head."

" Give the gentleman back his hat, Monica,"

said the Vicar. " You can be splendid just as well without it."

Monica did so. To tell the truth, she had suddenly lost interest in keeping her neighbour cool. For Trimmer just then was being removed from the ground, and she felt a wave of ecstasy pass through her at the sight. For now the twelfth man would be called on, Joe would play for England. If he were on the field, while only one ball was bowled, he would have played for England. She must be the first to embrace him and wish him luck. She sprang up and murmuring alternately " Heaven bless you, Joe " and " Excuse me "—for she was at once a pious and polite girl—forced her way into the pavilion. She had no right to be there at all, but in the general confusion no-one stopped her. She made her way directly, as though by instinct, to the players' dressing-room. It was empty. No sign of Joe. His flannels hung there, his blazer, his Glebeshire cap, but of her beloved man himself no sign. She looked round her in dismay. Where could he be ? Surely he was not going to miss this heaven-sent opportunity.

Just then Norman Blood entered, looking worried and anxious. She ran to him at once.

" Norman, where is Joe ? "

His answer amazed her.

" He is, at present," he said, sadly shaking his head, " bound and gagged in the heart of a minor county called Loamshire."

" Then," she gasped, " he will not be able to field."

" No," replied Norman. " I am sorry for that because he is a noble-hearted youth and saved me from those villains."

" But who will field now instead of Trimmer ? "

" That is just what I have to decide. Perhaps one of the ground staff."

Then it was that Monica had the inspiration of her life.

" Norman," she cried with shining eyes, " let me take his place."

The English captain looked at her in amazement.

" You, a girl ! "

" Why not ? " she pleaded. " You remember how we used to play together in the old days at the Manor House. You always said what a good fielder I was, even though we used a soft ball. I will put on Joe's things. No-one will know."

" But why do you want to field, Monica ? "

" I love Joe," she said earnestly. " Father said we could be married, if Joe played for England. Perhaps if I play it will do as well. Joe has sacrificed his chance to save you. Do this in return. Oh, Norman, please. I promise I won't drop a catch."

And so presently the crowd saw Norman return accompanied by a slim figure in white flannels. They could not see the fair bobbed hair tucked beneath a Glebeshire cap, and the word went round, " That's Prestwick."

As they walked to the wicket Monica had her second inspiration. She and Norman had not partaken together in a game of cricket since those distant days, when she was a child with golden ringlets. In those days she had nearly always contrived to get a wicket when the efforts of the butler, the gardener and the chauffeur had failed . . .

" Norman," she exclaimed, " I believe I could get Lethbridge out. May I bowl ? "

But Norman replied,

" No, the twelfth man cannot bowl. Besides Truth must finish his over."

" May I whisper to Truth ? " she pleaded prettily. " I've got a lovely idea."

He shrugged his shoulders.

" Very well."

The great crowd saw the slim figure in the Glebeshire cap approach Truth and speak to him.   But they could not see the amazed look which came upon Truth's face, nor hear him suddenly mutter,

" By George, I'll try it."

" It nearly always comes off," replied the slim figure.   " It takes people by surprise."

The crowd saw the slim figure run lightly in the direction of mid wicket where she was to take Trimmer's place.   They saw Truth run up to bowl.   And then they witnessed the final sensation of that amazing day.   Truth tossed the ball high into the air.   Higher than anyone present ever remembered to have seen a ball bowled.   Up and up and up soared that extraordinary ball and presently amid a profound hush began to descend.   Lethbridge, as was subsequently revealed upon the News reel, watched its gradually accelerating approach with feelings which veered from amazement and contempt to apprehension and sudden dismay.   The crowd saw the greatest batsman of modern times stand undecided and then leap suddenly backwards, as the ball threatened to descend upon his head. They saw him swing his bat in a last desperate swipe. Then a great shout went up, as it was seen that the wicket was shattered. Lethbridge was out. Bowled Truth, 65. England had won the match by one run.

Instantly pandemonium broke loose. While the cricketers grabbed up the stumps and ran for shelter, the vast crowd, almost delirious with excitement, surged towards the pavilion. There they remained cheering and shouting for the players. Every member of both teams —save one who had mysteriously vanished— appeared and was applauded. Norman Blood and Lethbridge shook hands. Norman Blood made a speech, in which he referred to the gallantry of his team under what were practically war conditions. Finally Lethbridge spoke,

" It has been a remarkable match," he said simply. " It's a pity the best team did not win. But still everyone is very fit."

Not for nearly an hour did the vast crowd begin to stream away.

*   *   *

All England rejoiced that evening. In country districts beacons were lit. In London there were scenes of almost hysterical enthusiasm. The west-end was filled with a cheering throng. A huge crowd surrounded the Blood town house in Sleek Street and would not be satisfied until Norman had appeared upon the balcony and spoken a few words.

The sound of cheering penetrated into the bedroom in the Blood house where lay Joe Prestwick, conscious now and, in fact, little the worse for his night's adventures.

Monica sat beside him, agog with womanly sympathy. A profusion of grapes and flowers lay at his bedside and his head was lightly bandaged, not because there was anything the matter with it, but because Monica was in that sort of mood.

" Lie still, my heroic one," she said, gently stroking his bandaged forehead. " Shall I bring you a glass of water or change your pillows ? "

" You've just changed them," said Joe.

" A woman loves to serve," she replied simply. " Keep lying still and I will bring you a cold-water compress."

" Monica," he said at last somewhat feebly, when she had performed this womanly act with loving care.

" Well ? "

" You know, don't you, that I had to do what I did ? I couldn't leave the Skipper in the hands of those villains."

" Of course not, Joe."

" But because of it, you see, I never played for England."

" No," replied Monica, and then at last she brought herself to break her wonderful news, " but I did."

Joe stared incredulously,

" You ! "

" I took your place, Joe. It was I who went on the field as twelfth man, and I who advised Truth to bowl that donkey drop."

Quickly she explained to the bewildered Joe what had happened.

" And so you see," she concluded, " one of us has played for England. I'm sure Father wouldn't mind which it was."

" Monica," he said weakly, " you're wonderful."

" I think I am rather," she replied softly. " Lie still, dear Joe, while I take your temperature and then I will put your arm in a sling."

" One woe doth tread upon another's heels."

*Hamlet, or The Prince who lacked the Test Match
Temperament.*   Shakespeare (W.) (Warwickshire).

AFTERMATH

Upon the following morning the Press rose to the occasion with unanimity and gusto. Such headlines as **BLOODSHED AT THE OVAL, STORM OF LEAD INTERRUPTS LAST OVER** flared across front pages. Moreover, the events of the previous night had now become generally known and were suitably related.

**FURTHER OUTRAGES
ENGLAND'S CAPTAIN KIDNAPPED
PRESTWICK (J.) AT BAY IN LONELY COTTAGE
N. BLOOD'S DASH FOR THE OVAL**

" Emissaries of the Bad Men kidnapped N. Blood, England's popular captain, last night at the point of a revolver. But for the gallantry and presence of mind of Prestwick (J.), the well-known Glebeshire spin-bowler, it is extremely doubtful whether N. Blood would have been present at the Oval for yesterday's play. Such is the latest development in the story of the most amazing Test Match of modern times . . ."

Joe, interviewed upon the subject, gave a modest and manly account of his part in the affair, which appeared in many papers.

An enterprising reporter on the staff of the *Daily Haywire* made a dash for Glebeshire to interview the gallant man's aged parents, but found them so rude as to be completely unintelligible. Mr. Prestwick, in fact, when approached in breezy journalistic fashion, merely uttered a low brutish snarl and, waving a pitchfork with considerable menace, observed,

" Thee mün püsh off, läd. Main gürt quick thee mün, bör."

A statement which the baffled and somewhat terrified reporter subsequently amplified.

" Prestwick's venerable father, whom I found engaged in simple rural tasks, stated,

" ' My wife and I are proud of our boy's indomitable pluck. He has always been a courageous lad and we knew that he would never fail in a crisis. From our hearts we say " Well played, Prestwick ! " ' "

It was the *Morning Scream,* which among the welter of sensational events, hit upon yet another headline.

MYSTERY CRICKETER
WHO TOOK PRESTWICK'S PLACE?

" Amidst the unprecedented scenes of confusion and bloodshed which occurred at the Oval yesterday there is one question which has as yet to be answered. Who was the player who took Prestwick's place as twelfth man? When the gallant Trimmer was carried from the field, someone took his place while the final ball was bowled. It was generally supposed that this was Prestwick, the twelfth man, but at that time Prestwick lay bound and gagged in a deserted cottage on the Loamshire moors. Who was this Mystery Fieldsman who took his place and subsequently vanished? Enquiries among eminent cricketers throw no light upon the mystery . . ."

So the sensations followed one another, but gradually the principal feeling of the country became one of wrath that the villains who had engineered this series of outrages upon the national life should escape unscathed. The ominous question began to be asked : WHAT IS THE YARD DOING?

A great wave of unpopularity almost submerged the Big Six. The Press thundered against them ; everywhere honest citizens could be heard deploring the incompetence which had allowed a small band of men to defy a nation. The criminal classes, rising happily to the unique occasion, organized a monster demonstration. It was a heartening sight to see old lags of all ages and sexes marching in procession with banners bearing such slogans as,

**THE BIG SIX MUST GO
DON'T TRUST THAT TWISTER POSSE
THE POLICE IS ROTTEN**

A vast and enthusiastic meeting was addressed by Jim the Basher, Club-foot Arthur and other well-known criminals. A proposal put forward by Nutty Williams, the distinguished " con-man ", that the Metropolitan police should be instantly disbanded was greeted with acclaim.

In official circles the matter was regarded as grave. The Home Secretary spoke seriously to the Commissioner, who in his turn spoke seriously to the Assistant-Commissioner.

The Assistant-Commissioner addressed the Big Six.

" You'll have to go, boys, if you don't find out something soon."

" We are working at the highest pressure,"

said Steady as a Rock Posse glumly. " My dramatic dash to Loamshire would have caught them if they hadn't had that airplane."

" We are relentlessly pursuing every clue," said Who Dies if England Lives Narkley.

" All ports are being watched," said And What is More You'll be a Man, my Son Darby.

" That is not good enough," snapped the Assistant-Commissioner. " The public want someone arrested. And you can't altogether blame them."

" I don't quite see what we can do if we resign," muttered Dogged Does It Cordon.

" You'll have to learn up a few jokes and become amateur detectives," replied the Assistant-Commissioner coldly.

The Big Six shuddered as one man.

*   *   *

But the Big Six were not after all called upon to resign. For almost before the words " Bloodshed " and " Mystery Cricketer " had disappeared from the headlines a new sensation came into being, which distracted public opinion. There arose the fierce conflict of opinion which ultimately passed into Cricket history as the Great Donkey Drop Controversy.

The controversy began when the Imperian Board of Management decided that the final ball of the match which had bowled Lethbridge was not a legitimate ball at all. It was, they maintained, unlike any ball previously bowled in international cricket. Having decided upon this they immediately sent a cable to the M.C.C.

" Board considers ball which bowled Lethbridge foul and unsportsmanlike device. Stop. Suggest match should be played again."

To which the M.C.C. sent what was generally spoken of as a statesmanlike reply,

" Nothing in Laws of Cricket forbids use of Donkey Drop. Stop. In any case Board of Management not present and could not possibly have seen it."

The Board then cabled,

" Demand replay of entire match. Stop. Otherwise regret shall refuse to play you again. Stop. Donkey Drops are not cricket."

To which the M.C.C. replied in somewhat less statesmanlike fashion,

" Rubbish."

This, as the Press neatly pointed out, was deadlock.

Opinion all over the country was sharply divided. Letters and articles upon the subject flooded the Press. Lethbridge himself refused to make any comment except that he was still very fit. Truth would say nothing except that the idea of bowling this unusual ball had been put into his head by the now famous Mystery Cricketer, whom he had never seen before or since. Norman Blood in an interview, while refusing to comment upon the identity of the Mystery Cricketer, pointed out very sensibly that the umpire was the only judge of whether a ball was fair or not. It was subsequently revealed, however, that after the first day the places of the umpires had been taken by two well-known secret service men who knew little or nothing about the game. This heightened the general confusion.

The controversy raged. Everywhere the question was heatedly discussed. Crowds flocked to the cinemas to witness the flight of the historic ball. It was shown in slow motion, a process which took several minutes. Every detail was displayed, the solemn ascent, the interminable descent, the varying expressions on Lethbridge's face, the final laborious shattering of his wicket.   At that climax the packed audiences clapped or booed according to their views upon the Great Donkey Drop Controversy.

The situation grew more serious.   A thunderous article by Mr. Clinton Dimskull, the ex-cabinet minister, appeared in the *Evening Flagpost*, in which he urged that a Ministry of Cricket be forthwith set up with himself as Minister.   In a noble passage he wrote,

" I shall get back over this crisis.   Mark my words.   The unthinking may declare that I have tried to cash in over the last three crises and failed, but this time there shall be no faltering.   My great powers shall no longer rust in disuse.   The nation may not think that it wants me, but it does.   I am coming back."

The situation became acute.   The M.C.C. and the Board of Management ceased cabling each other and remained firm.   Once again crowds in Downing Street saw the Colonial Secretary hurrying to confer with the Prime Minister.

Avoiding such controversial topics as the rival merits of Prestwick and Swerver the two statesmen took counsel.   It was decided that a Committee of eminent men should be set up to consider the best way out of the impasse. The Committee met, and after several days of watching the slow-motion ascent and descent of the now celebrated donkey drop and Lethbridge's final ineffectual swipe, produced their report. It proposed a compromise, namely that an Act of Parliament should instantly be passed, proclaiming the match a draw.

Parliament was summoned early. A tense and crowded House debated the matter. In the Strangers' Gallery many distinguished figures were to be seen, including those of Sir Timothy Blood, Q. E. D. Marjoribanks and R. S. V. P. Hatstock.

The Bill was not passed without much hostile criticism. After the Prime Minister had, in person, outlined its main provisions and stated that if necessary he was ready to face a General Election on this issue, the leader of the Opposition in a fighting speech asked amid cheers from his supporters, " Since when has it been the custom for visiting cricket teams to dictate to the mother country ? " How, he went on to demand, could our gallant bowlers do themselves justice, unless they felt that they had the weight of the country behind them ? He took his stand, he said, punning happily, beside Truth and Truth should prevail. In his peroration he pointed out that the tactics adopted by Truth were roughly those of William the Conqueror at the Battle of Hastings. Had anyone at that time or since drawn attention to those tactics as unsporting? (An Hon. Member, "William was a Frenchman. French cricket is quite a different game.")

The debate continued.

Mr. Clinton Dimskull brought all his great oratorical powers to the suggestion that a Ministry of Cricket should instantly be formed. The Government, in his opinion, had consistently mishandled the Test Match from the very moment when Blood and Lethbridge tossed. Apart altogether from the burning immediate question of the donkey drop, there had been unusual and unpleasant incidents which had undermined public confidence and which could never have arisen if there had been a Ministry with a strong Minister.

The setting up of a Ministry was also advocated by Mr. Leek-Thomas, that indomitable and picturesque veteran, who differed only from Mr. Dimskull in proposing that he himself should be appointed Minister.

" I have," he declared in a particularly striking passage, " been trying to cash in on a crisis far longer than my right hon. friend, nor is my ignorance of cricket any greater than his. You see before you a venerable, if tiresome old man, who yearns to appear once again in the limelight. I put it to the generosity of the House that my great powers should be utilized in preference to his."

The House was genuinely moved by the pathos of this appeal and the veteran was sympathetically applauded, much to the annoyance of Mr. Clinton Dimskull, who was heard to shout aloud the word " Humbug ! ".

Many other speeches were made, both for and against the Bill. Mr. Gripe (Lib. North Wessex) pointed out that a timeless Test Match could not, by its very nature, result in a draw. If the Government were determined to throw away the victory achieved by our gallant men under conditions of unparalleled hardship and even danger, the match must be accounted a tie. Mr. Stockchest (Cons. N. Loamshire) said that when a cricket match was over, it was over. The phrase " it is not cricket " had embedded itself in the national consciousness. What, the hon. member enquired passionately, would become of our national heritage if the results of cricket matches could be altered at will ?

Mr. Gumbridge (Lib.) put forward the suggestion that in future, Test Matches should be played at Geneva under the ægis of the League. This suggestion caused a considerable uproar among hon. members. From the Strangers' Gallery Sir Timothy was heard to shout wildly that he would rather see the entire House of Commons dead at his feet than that a Test Match should be played on foreign soil. Q. E. D. Marjoribanks was also heard to say that League cricket was already in existence and was ruining the game.

The uproar having subsided Mr. Titmuss (Lab.) asked if the Government had any information to give the House upon the question of the now famous Mystery Cricketer who was reported to be responsible for the entire donkey drop business.

Mr. Biter (Lab.) said that the Government would be better employed after the recent Test Match in safeguarding the lives of the nation's cricketers than in worrying over little points of etiquette.

Mr. Hunterbotham (Lib.) asked if the

Government had considered the effect of the Bill on Truth's bowling average.

Sir Herbert Boyling (Cons.) said that he had played cricket for two schools, his university and his county and had never in his long experience encountered a donkey drop.

Mr. Croak (Soc.) said that if you wanted to win a match, you had to use any means you could. For his part he advocated the use by England's bowlers of donkey drops, sneaks, grubs or any other kind of ball that seemed likely to get the opposing batsmen out. If the bowler was able to bowl before the batsman was ready, so much the better. (Cries of " Shame " and counter cheers. A voice from the Strangers' Gallery, " That man is a socialist.")

Mrs. Crowhurst (Lab.) drew the attention of the House to the fact that matches were now played between the women of England and Imperia. In her opinion it was a pity that if women could play cricket without all this fuss, men could not do the same. (Ironical laughter.)

Mr. Sturrocker (Ind.) who was well-known to be the biggest nuisance in either House, enquired, " Would it matter very greatly if there were no further matches between England

and Imperia, or indeed any cricket matches at all ? "

Indignant shouts of " Withdraw " greeted this question.

(An Hon. Member, " It's only Sturrocker." Groans and laughter.)

The Colonial Secretary finally wound up the debate. He categorically denied reports of a Cabinet Split and his own resignation. These he described as malicious inventions. With regard to the recently concluded Test Match, he admitted that there were unsatisfactory features in the situation—the failure to capture the Bad Men, the lack of information regarding the Mystery Cricketer—but he urged hon. members to take a broad view. Supposing in two years' time when we were due to send a team to Imperia, the Imperians refused to play ? Would not hon. members who had voted against the Bill reproach themselves bitterly ? Surely it was better to show a little generosity now and regard the offending donkey drop as never having been bowled ? He announced that in order to spare any hurt to Truth's feelings, the Government had arranged with his county to give him a special benefit match next season. (Prolonged Government cheers.)

It was at a late hour that the House divided, the Government ultimately securing a handsome majority. A Bill was approved, accounting the Oval Test Match a draw, and ordaining that Lethbridge's score should, by Act of Parliament, go down to history as 65 not out.

At the conclusion of this long and wearying debate the Prime Minister was returning home, when on the pavement outside the House he encountered a paper boy. It was not often that he found the information displayed by news-bills either novel or encouraging. But this particular one caused him to smile and murmur, in a relieved voice,

" Thank Heaven for that ! "

The poster said quite boldly, **FOOTBALL STARTS AGAIN.**

*   *   *

One afternoon, not long after the great Donkey Drop Debate in the House, Sawn-off Carlo and Ralph the Disappointment sat awaiting the coming of the Professor. They sat before the same café where details of the Test Match Crime had been first discussed. All about them moved the same fashionably attired crowd of spies, financiers, film stars, international crooks and others. The same half-heard fragments of conversation floated through the sunlit air.

" The Minister of the Interior, *mon cher comte*, dines tonight at my villa. It is unnecessary that he should leave it alive . . ."

" Ten million dollars is my final offer, Swindleheim. Otherwise the deal is off . . ."

" She's got the ice with her, I tell you, Pug. We can lay our hands on it tonight. . . ."

The two men before the café waited almost in silence, taking no notice of the brilliant crowd. A certain melancholy seemed to sit upon them.

Said Sawn-off Carlo presently, shifting his gum,

" I guess, brother, this ball-game crime is not so good. We shan't see no dough. I guess these International saps are sore the English guys win this game."

Ralph the Disappointment shook his head sadly.

" It was a mad thing to attempt. I knew we should fail."

Presently the Professor appeared walking towards them through the gay crowd. He was dressed as on the occasion of their former meeting, a yachting cap was set rakishly on his dome-like forehead. As usual he greeted his colleagues as chance acquaintances. Then having seated himself at their table and made certain that they were not under observation, he furtively handed to each a bulky packet.

" The proceeds, my friends, of our recent trip to England."

The two gazed at him in surprise.

" Gee, Boss ! " exclaimed Sawn-off Carlo in delight. " Say, do these International punks hand out the dough okay and hunky-dory ? "

" As you see, Carlo."

" Ain't that swell ? "

" But don't they realize," asked Ralph the Disappointment slowly, " that we were defeated, that we failed ? "

The Professor permitted his lips to twitch in a smile.

" I must admit, my friends," he said, " that thanks in the first place to Carlo's stupidity and in the second place to his inadequate marksmanship, I was prepared to regard the affair as that unique thing, a failure upon my part."

" Aw, say, Boss," protested Sawn-off Carlo, " I guess if them military guys hadn't started shooting us up I'd 'a' left that Oval plenty full of cadavers."

"It seems, however," the Professor continued, ignoring Sawn-off's interruption, "that I underrated both the madness of the English and the insane complications of this game of crickets. It appears that after our somewhat hurried departure from the Oval an English sportsman by the name of Truth outwitted the principal native, Lethbridge, by bowling in an illegitimate manner. There is a kind of ball known as a donkey drop, of which I must confess I had not previously heard, since it is not mentioned by Mr. L. E. G. Glance in his monumental work. The delivery of this ball has plunged the British Empire into the utmost confusion. Only urgent action by the English Government, who have declared the match to be a draw, has prevented disaster. My employers, who as I told you represent important International Interests, are greatly delighted at the turn of events and have congratulated me most warmly. The affair may, therefore, despite certain hitches in our arrangements, be said to have concluded in a blaze of success."

Sawn-off Carlo shook his head in bewilderment.

"I always knew them guys was phoney," he said at last, "but this sure beats everything."

"And now, my friends," the Professor paused to light one of his thin cigars, while behind his great round spectacles his eyes shone with a queer eager light, "as to our future operations. I have devised a novel and interesting scheme which I think will prove to be tolerably lucrative. I propose, in short, that we should kidnap the infant daughter of Socrates F. Grünbaum, the well-known millionaire, who is at present upon a visit to Europe from the United States. Socrates F. Grünbaum is, I understand, devoted to his infant daughter, and would be willing to pay handsomely . . ."

The thin precise voice spoke on, outlining details of his plans.

When at last he had finished, it might have been observed that for the first time in many weeks a smile crossed the morose face of Ralph the Disappointment.

"Thank Heaven!" he said with emotion. "At last a crime in which I can partake without feeling an outcast among men."

233

. " The Bride lightly swung a tasteful bouquet of the Glebeshire colours and a good time was had by all."

From the *Glebeshire Clarion*

WEDDING BELLS

It was a pretty wedding, which was held that autumn day in the old church of Wattlecombe Ducis.

Many distinguished cricketers were present, including Sir Timothy and Q. E. D. Marjoribanks, Norman Blood who officiated as best man, Hugh and Crigh, Truth and Teddy Trimmer, as well as almost all the members of the Glebeshire team, who subsequently formed a guard of honour, the happy pair walking from the church beneath an arch of crossed cricket bats. Only one minor mishap marred the proceedings. Monica's saintly old father, in his excitement at seeing so many famous cricketers among his congregation, took with him *Wisden's Almanac* for 1906 from the Vestry instead of his prayer book, and was forced to return and rectify the mistake before the service could proceed.

Afterwards the company repaired to the wedding breakfast at the Earthy Peasant. Immense jollity prevailed. Champagne flowed like water. Here again a slight awkwardness occurred. The elder Prestwicks were unused to champagne and became in consequence ruder than ever. A well-known Glebeshire amateur was felt to put the matter in a nutshell when he inquired,

" I say, couldn't that peasant put his hand in front of his mouth, when that happens ? "

Nothing, however, was allowed to damp the general high spirits. Great excitement was caused when it was disclosed that among the numerous telegrams of congratulations was one from Lethbridge.

" Heartiest congratulations," the great man had written. " Everyone is very fit."

Several speeches were made. Sir Timothy, after a protracted review of the cricket season which included references to the burning Donkey Drop Controversy and the activities of the Bad Men, suddenly and unexpectedly proposed the health of the bride and bridegroom. Referring to the latter, he said in felicitous terms,

" Whatever the Selection Committee may think of his merits, there is no doubt that he has bowled at least one maiden over."

A somewhat startled pause greeted this re-

mark. Then it was realized that Sir Timothy
had made a joke. The rafters rang.

Speeches were also made by Joe and Norman
as well as by the saintly old vicar.

" This is a very happy day for me," said that
good old man. " I am proud to see my daughter married to an honest young fellow and
an excellent spin-bowler like Joe Prestwick.
(Tremendous applause.) Joe has finished up
the season with a bowling average of which
any wife may be proud. I am sure she will
make him a good wife. I like to think of her
in the years to come, putting Joe's bats to bed
and afterwards oiling his children. At one
time the foolish girl was, for some reason, anxious to marry R. T. Wright who was in the
Cambridge eleven of 1902 (a somewhat puzzled
silence), but I was able to point out to her
that R. T. Wright, though an admirable
batsman, died in 1927 and so she was forced
to abandon this rather stupid idea and marry
Joe Prestwick." (A further puzzled silence,
broken by loud applause at the mention of
Joe's name.)

The old man then recounted ball by ball the
events of the University Match of 1884, and
finally sat down amid great cheering.

Q. E. D. Marjoribanks then spoke, but as the popular veteran, having consumed a great deal of champagne, appeared to be under the impression that he was attending the annual dinner of the Eastshire C.C., much of what he said was irrelevant.

Subsequently there was dancing in the village hall. The hall presented a gay scene, cricketers whose names were household words dancing with rustic wenches. Sir Timothy gallantly led off with Mrs. Prestwick senior, but almost immediately found her so rude that he abandoned the attempt. Instead he led her to a seat and told her the story of the epic catch made by B. G. M. Seedways in 1901.

" It was upon the old cricket ground at Buckstead Wells. You perhaps do not remember it ? "

" Näy, rëckon önt never."

" Quite," said Sir Timothy, " oh, quite. Well, the Gentlemen of Glebeshire were batting and Slogger Peaboom made a tremendous drive. We all thought it was going for six, when we saw Bertie Seedways racing round the boundary. Simply racing. He got there. Bertie Seedways got there, believe it or not, madam, and he jumped up and held it.

By gad, he held it. Never saw such a thing in my life."

Mrs. Prestwick, who had listened throughout with an expression of bestial stupidity, replied,

" Ee, thicky wör main gürt, räckon."

" Quite," replied Sir Timothy a little dashed. " Well, if you will excuse me, madam, I see the Vicar beckoning."

" I say," he remarked later to the Vicar, " that old woman is really frightfully rude."

" It comes of wringing a bare living from the soil," replied the Vicar. " Nothing can be done about it."

" I suppose not," replied Sir Timothy. " Well, I think I'll go home now. Good night, Vicar."

The gay festivities went on until long after sunset. The moon shone over Wattlecombe Ducis when at last amid showers of confetti and cries of " Good Luck ! " Monica and Joe set off for their simple home, which was appropriately called " Googly Cottage ".

" Are you happy, spin-bowler o' mine ? " asked Monica as they walked through the starlit evening.

" Wildly happy, my little Mystery Cricketer,"

241

replied Joe, who was beginning to get the knack
of this sort of thing.

" And you'll never, never grow tired of your
little wife ? "

" Never," replied Joe ardently. " Besides,"
he pointed out sensibly, " it's not so very long
until next cricket season."

" And in four years' time," added Monica,
" the Imperians will be here again. Perhaps," she added prettily, " by that time we
shall have one or more little spin-bowlers
tumbling on our simple lawn."

" I hope they'll be left-handed," said Joe.
" It helps."

" I suppose it does."

" Why, of course. You see, if a chap bowls
round the wicket . . ."

The happy pair walked on, dreaming happily
of the future.

Let us sing
In praise of Spring.
     (Hey nonny no, tra-la.)
Shepherd's pipe and swallows wing
As the months their message bring,
Advertisement's a gladsome thing.
     (Green grow the public o').
On the dove the iris burns,
And a young man's fancy turns
To the royalties he earns.
     (Loud sing ballyhoo.)
O heaven-sent prophet to th' untutored mind
If Sellers come, can Spring be far behind?
     (" Hey nonny no ", " Come, Shepherds,
     come ", " An unusually sensitive novel ", and
     other odd cries.)

        From *Ballads of the Seasons*, or *The Man*
                Who Was Thursday Evening

EXTRACT FROM THE DIARY OF SAWN-OFF CARLO

So it seems like after all this Test Match crime is okay and hunky-dory, because these English guys are sure phoney, and it seems after me and Ralph and the Big Shot ease off in our airplane, one of these cricketing palookas tries to pull a fast one, and this gets the Imperian guys mad and so the British Empire is almost disrupted after all, and the International bozos hand out the dough and everything is okay and hunky-dory.

But the Big Shot is sore, because he says I can't shoot good enough to hit the State Building and other old-fashioned cracks, and this is a great big wound to my manly pride, because it is okay ironing out them cricketing palookas, but it is not so good when certain military characters start something and we get the heat. So Ralph the Disappointment says these military characters are certain saps called the Goids, and Ralph the Disappointment says these Goids are well known to one and all to

be the cats slumber wear in military guys. So
one of these Goids gives me the well-known
stream of lead through my fedora, and this is
not so good. So we scram and I say I guess
we left plentya cadavers among those cricketing
palookas, but the Big Shot says I only hit one
guy, which was a sap by the name of Trimmer,
and it seems this Trimmer guy did not hand in
his dinner-pail, but was only a bit sore about
the leg, which is not so good.

So Ralph the Disappointment says he never
thinks this crime would be so good because it
is well-known to one and all that these English
guys are screwy over this ball game, and I too
do not think it is so good, because I see no more
of Flash Alice and I guess me and that dame
coulda gotten together in a big way. Because
had that frail swell curves and plentya this and
that or had she ? Oh, boy, I'm telling you.

So now the Big Shot is thinking up a new
crime, because that guy can't rest unless he is
thinking up a crime. So this crime is to kidnap
the little daughter of Socrates F. Grünbaum
the millionaire, because the Boss says that it is
well known that it is pain and grief to million-
aires to have their little daughters kidnapped,
and maybe they hand out the dough in a big

way. But I guess this crime is not so good, since it is well-known to one and all that us killers get very sentimental about little dolls, especially when these little dolls have curly hair and blue eyes and a good line in childish prattle, because there is nothing makes us guys sentimental in a big way like childish prattle. And especially if this curly headed doll says " Tell me a fairy story, Mr. Stranger " when you are going to start something it is not so good, because we get thinking about our innocent childish days and our dear old mommas and Christmas, and then we get very sentimental indeed. And maybe we take the doll on our knee and pull a few childish cracks while her loving poppa, which is none other than Socrates F. Grünbaum, calls up the cops, and even if the curly headed doll says "Mr. Stranger is such a kind man," well maybe the dicks don't believe it. And that is not so good.

So I think maybe I'll give the Boss the dead pan and give up crime. I think maybe I'll be an author, since it is well-known to one and all that any saps who can read fall for tough books, especially if these tough books are written by a guy with a great big hearta gold and in this way I make plentya dough. I am reading in a

London newspaper how some literary citizen is making a speech at a literary luncheon, and it seems this literary citizen is some palooka's book of the month. So I fall to thinking how proud my old momma would be in her bum apoitment house if her loving son is a literary citizen and makes highbrow cracks at luncheon to a lot of other literary bozos. And I guess a guy needn't go all sissy and give up shooting up other guys because he is a literary character, because it seems there are saps called publishers and other palookas called reviewers. So I guess if I threaten to iron out one or two of these characters I'll be someone's book of the month like this other literary citizen, and so I'll make plentya dough and everything will be okay and hunky-dory.

So what?